Raven Queen

"A beautiful interpretation of the life of Lady Jane Grey, an iconic but misunderstood figure in history. This stunning and lyrical tale will hold readers captive and haunt them long after the last page has been turned."
Becky Stradwick, Borders

"An utterly fabulous read . . . Philippa Gregory for a younger audience."
Rachel Forward, Gardners Books

"Vivid and poetic, *Raven Queen* brings to life the power and menace of the Tudor Court."
Ann Turnbull

D1151253

Raven Queen

Pauline Francis

USBORNE

COVENTRY SCHOOLS LIBRARY SERVICE	
24-May-07	JF
PETERS	

For Rob

First published in the UK in 2007 by Usborne Publishing Ltd., Usborne House, 83-85 Saffron Hill, London EC1N 8RT, England. www.usborne.com

Copyright © Pauline Francis, 2007. All rights reserved.

The right of Pauline Francis to be identified as the author of this work has been asserted by her in accordance with the Copyright, Designs and Patents Act, 1988.

The name Usborne and the devices ♈ ⊕ are Trade Marks of Usborne Publishing Ltd.

All rights reserved. No part of this publication may be reproduced, stored in a retrieval system or transmitted in any form or by any means, electronic, mechanical, photocopying, recording or otherwise without the prior permission of the publisher.

A CIP catalogue record for this book is available from the British Library.

J MAMJJASOND/07   ISBN 9780746078808
Printed in Great Britain.

The Tudor family tree

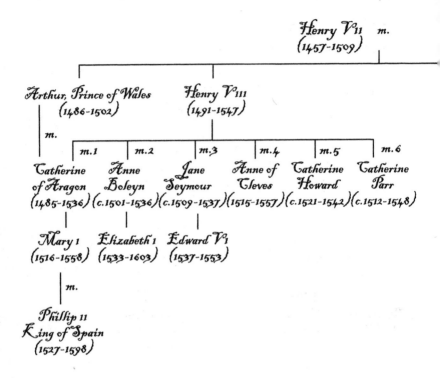

Henry VII
(1457-1509) m.

Arthur, Prince of Wales
(1486-1502)

Henry VIII
(1491-1547)

m.

m.1 m.2 m.3 m.4 m.5 m.6

Catherine of Aragon
(1485-1536)

Anne Boleyn
(c.1501-1536)

Jane Seymour
(c.1509-1537)

Anne of Cleves
(1515-1557)

Catherine Howard
(c.1521-1542)

Catherine Parr
(c.1512-1548)

Mary 1
(1516-1558)

Elizabeth 1
(1533-1603)

Edward VI
(1537-1553)

m.

Phillip 11
King of Spain
(1527-1598)

m. — married

# of Lady Jane Grey

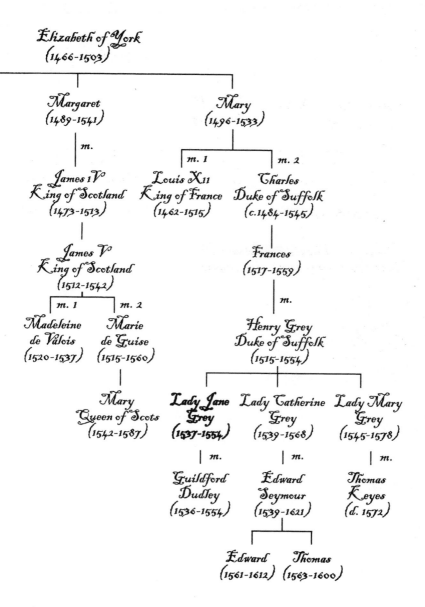

Elizabeth of York
(1466–1503)

Margaret
(1489–1541)
m.

James IV
King of Scotland
(1473–1513)

James V
King of Scotland
(1512–1542)
m. 1   m. 2

Madeleine
de Valois
(1520–1537)

Marie
de Guise
(1515–1560)

Mary
Queen of Scots
(1542–1587)

Mary
(1496–1533)
m. 1   m. 2

Louis XII
King of France
(1462–1515)

Charles
Duke of Suffolk
(c.1484–1545)

Frances
(1517–1559)
m.

Henry Grey
Duke of Suffolk
(1515–1554)

Lady Jane
Grey
(1537–1554)
m.

Lady Catherine
Grey
(1539–1568)
m.

Lady Mary
Grey
(1545–1578)
m.

Guildford
Dudley
(1536–1554)

Edward
Seymour
(1539–1621)

Thomas
Keyes
(d. 1572)

Edward
(1561–1612)

Thomas
(1563–1600)

1552
Leicestershire

Ned

I am not afraid to die.

I have walked the three miles from Leicester prison, tied to a horse carrying the two men who will hang me. Now they are sitting on the ground, swigging their ale before they begin their dirty work: one old, one young, but both toothless. And I know the young one is the wild one, the one to watch.

I drag my hands towards the pocket of my breeches

and finger the rosary beads hidden there, whispering, "Holy Mary, Mother of God, pray for us sinners now and at the hour of our death."

"Blood drinker!" the old one cries.

The young one sniggers. "Look at that! He's pleasuring himself before he dies! The devil makes work for idle hands."

No, I am not afraid to die. *Death is only a hobgoblin sent to frighten us in the night!* my father used to say. But although my mind is strong, my body betrays me. I wet myself. To my surprise, although the men wrinkle their noses, they make no mention of it.

Another thought consoles me. I shall see my mother for the first time in the new world that is waiting to welcome me. Then panic tightens my throat. How will she recognize me now that I am almost fully grown? I was only a baby when she died.

How stupid I am! *I* shall know *her* from the painting my father keeps of her in a locket: fair skin, fair hair and eyes soft brown like almonds dappled in an autumn sun.

"Was it worth it then, for an apple and a loaf o' bread?" the old one asks. "Doesn't your God tell you it's wrong to steal?"

I nod. "Yes, but it does not deserve death. '*Society must take responsibility for its thieves since our society forces thieving*'," I quote.

Their mouths gape.

I am almost light-hearted now as I carry on, "Have you not read *Utopia*, gentlemen? It is a very good book and I can heartily recommend it to you."

"Fancy words!" the old one hisses. He pushes the boy forward. "But they're no good to a condemned man. Get up there, lad!"

The apprentice springs onto the horse's back and my lips move in silent prayer. His friend sneers, "Too late for that!" and staggers to his feet, pushing me up onto the horse's back where I sway. The boy is already reaching for the noose above my head and, in a second, it lies heavy around my neck where it will soon squeeze the life out of me.

At least I shall hang in the beauty of the countryside

and I thank God for that. Dew glints early on the grass for the sun is already sinking, and above me the gallows is so new that I can smell its sweet sap.

"I like town hangings best!" the boy calls down to his friend. "All them people baying for blood, so to speak. Quiet gallows ain't my style."

"I forgive you both for the wrong you are about to do," I say quietly.

He takes a step back from me, almost losing his balance in his anger and I expect him to hit me, so I duck. As I stand up again, lurching like an acrobat I once saw, he leans forward, steadying himself until his eyes are level with mine. I can see myself in them: all tangled hair and beard. Almost a stranger.

He spits in my face.

I stand still, feeling the spittle slide down my forehead, sticking in my eyebrows and eyelashes. A skylark calls in the sky and I glance up, straining the rope. Then I laugh out loud. Dear God, my last sight of your beautiful creation has been dimmed by a hangman's spittle. Oh, I am weary of this world and

I long to lay down the burden of my life.

The horse rears and pricks its ears at the thud of hooves beyond the hedges. The boy jumps down and the men draw back, whispering. I cannot hear what they are saying although it is clear to me that they are disagreeing.

The old one insists, "I've been told to wait till sunset!"

"Who's going to know?" The boy's voice is mocking. "Except the ravens!"

"We'll wait, lad."

As the thudding shakes the ground, the hanging horse starts to snort and paw the air and the boy decides. "Time to meet your maker!" he shouts, slapping the horse's rump, and I look to heaven as it leaps forward without me, jolting my body.

A rush of air deep inside me.

And far off I hear my voice cry, "Mother!"

Jane

They were hanging a boy when Ellie and I rode past the gallows.

"Oh no, Ellie!" My voice rose to a wail of horror.

We thundered towards the dangling boy, lashing the hangmen away, letting his feet settle onto the back of my horse.

"Murdering dogs!" I shouted.

The men cursed and kicked as they tried to drag the boy back; but I scattered a handful of coins onto the ground and they scrambled on all fours for the greater share. Ellie pulled the noose over the boy's head and he flopped down behind me, choking and gasping.

Then we rode away.

His name was Ned and his stillness captivated me. Was he not afraid after what had happened? My heart was still drumming like my horse's hooves. What if my horse had stumbled, what if we had stopped to pick primroses in the hedgerows, what if...? I had never seen a hanging until today, although many times I had passed rotting bodies – swinging eyeless, noseless, lipless – and I shivered at the memory of them.

A few miles along the highway, where the trees began to thicken, he asked to be put down and part of me was glad because the stench seeping from his clothes sickened me; but I was surprised that his voice was soft, like a gentleman's.

He bowed and thanked me and turned to set off, tall

and proud, his eyes looking towards the trees already reddening in the sunset.

I could not bear to see him leave.

"Where will you go?" I called out.

He stopped and shrugged his shoulders.

"Can you use an axe?" I asked. Ellie mouthed NO at me and shook her head.

Ned rubbed the palm of his right hand and I saw that it was scarred silver. "I think so," he said. "It cannot be difficult."

Ellie rode up alongside me. She has been my nurse since my birth fourteen years ago and is never afraid to tell me when I am wrong. "I'm used to your stray birds and butterflies," she whispered, "but you've never brought back a stray boy before. What will your father say?"

"He is in London!" I whispered back. Then aloud, "I can find you work as a woodman, Ned. Come with us. It is not far."

He nodded.

He walked the rest of the way and we did not speak again until we passed through the gates of Bradgate

Hall. My heart sank when they closed behind me, trapping me in a loneliness so deep that I wanted to cry out.

Visitors usually gasp with pleasure when they first arrive. It is thought to be one of the finest houses in Leicestershire; but Ned gazed past its red brick towers, past its gardens soon to be brimming with fruit and blossom, past the stream which fed water pipes to the kitchen – to the darkening trees beyond.

"I like a forest best at dusk when birds cloud the sky," he said suddenly.

I glanced down at him. And now that he was standing closer to me, I no longer saw his tangled hair and grimy skin – only the smile that lit up his face.

Who *was* he?

Ned

I did not ask her to save me. I did not want to be saved.
And she certainly would have left me dangling there if
she had known how I prayed to my God.

I cannot stop looking at her, perched high on her
horse, her slender face alive with flashing eyes. Her hair
is glorious, streaming out behind her, red-gold.

I told her my name, but I dare not ask hers.

"Jane," her companion says. "She is Lady Jane Grey and she is usually shy with strangers. I wonder what has loosened her tongue today!"

"A stranger who wets himself with fear," I reply. "That is enough to loosen anybody's tongue." My cheeks redden with shame at my choice of words, but she roars with laughter.

I tremble as I walk beside them. I am entering the gates of the Greys – one of the most powerful Protestant families in England.

Statue smashers and blasphemers. My father's words echo in my head. That's what he used to call those of the new faith. He could not bring himself to use the word Protestant. Statue smashers because they hate painted statues. Blasphemers because they refuse to accept that the bread and wine change into Christ's body and blood during Mass.

I shall be safe. Who would look for me in such a place? I need not stay long. Yes, it will suit me to stay.

❊   ❊   ❊

I share a room above the bakehouse – which lies between the kitchen and the walled garden – with Jack, one of the gamekeepers. He is only a year older than me but his arms are muscular, his back broad. He calls me "boy", although I have turned sixteen and grown tall since I left Lincoln. But although I have grown tall on the outside, I know that inside anger and fear have stunted me.

Jack lets me sleep where the wall is warmed by the oven below. And he shows me the creatures he has snared in the forest, dangling them proudly in front of me.

How will I have the strength to cut and chop? My body is bony after living rough for so long. Thomas, the head woodman, scratches his head in thought as he looks me up and down. Then he gives me an axe. As I take it, its blade pulls me towards the ground and when I aim at the wood, I miss, wrenching every muscle. Pain darts through the scar on my palm. Then I try again. It is a better blow although it jars my body.

Thomas's axe flashes next to me like a flame as he shows me what to do. "A forest is ne'er fully grown," he says. "Its heads are allus being lopped. It's allus stunted by death."

I nod, straining to understand his dialect.

"I don't stand still, Ned," he laughs, "or they'll chop me down."

If he does take me on I shall have my work cut out, I know that. I have never done any physical labour.

"Come on, lad, put your back into it!" Thomas's voice is impatient. "There's many a lad round 'ere would be glad of the job."

I try harder. Sweat stains my shirt and every muscle strains as I struggle to find the rhythm. But when it comes at last, I cannot imagine any other way of working. The swish of the blade and the sway of my body empty my head of all thoughts, and the sap scents my skin with a perfume that the stream does not wash away.

Gnarled hands shake mine in welcome. "Aye, lad, I'll take thee. I'm glad to have an extra pair of hands.

Springtime's busy. Prunin' and choppin' and repairin' the damage from t'winter storms."

That evening, I sit on the doorstep of the bakehouse, catching the last light to read. Jack watches me, irritated by my silence. "I could teach you to read," I say gently, "then you could—"

His rough cheeks redden. "I could *what*? I don't need no books to set snares. I don't need no books to shoot. What good is books to me?"

"You could read the Bible now it's written in English," I reply. "Don't you want a better life, Jack?"

"There ain't no better life for me." He laughs in my face then. "Or for you."

And he cools towards me.

The forest calms me. It is called Charnwood and it is the biggest forest in Leicestershire. A hill rises in the west – Beacon Hill, Thomas tells me – and from the top, on a clear day, you can see Lincoln Cathedral. But I do not hear anything else that Thomas says then. I can only see our house in my mind, clinging to the hillside above the river. I can even smell its damp stone.

It is the most beautiful spring I have ever seen. Bluebells push through the earth and every leaf is unfolding bright green, and light flashes through them onto the forest floor.

One morning, when showers grey the skies and soak the wood, Jack trudges past to check his snares and I call out good day as I raise my axe. He stops to watch. I can see him from the corner of my eye, nudging Thomas's elbow and smiling. Rain drips down the handle of the axe, and down my nose into my mouth. I hesitate too long. The handle is slippery and I miss the branch, losing my axe and toppling full length into the mud. I taste its dankness on my lips.

I cannot find my footing, but Jack walks on, shoulders shaking as he laughs, and it is Thomas who pulls me out. I should laugh, I know. It would be better for me. But I cannot.

"Thee 'as to learn to take a joke, lad," Thomas says.

My heart races. "Jack has taken against me lately. I thought he would be a good friend."

Thomas pats the tree in front of us, one of the biggest oaks in that part of the forest. "This is my friend," he says. "A tree'll never let thee down."

As servants, we fare well. Ale and meat in the kitchen at first light, cheese and bread warm from the oven to take to work, and sometimes an apple, and, at last light, more bread and ale. I have never tasted ale before, although I do not admit to this and I grow to like its bitter cool.

My body fills out in the first few days and my arms strengthen, and soon I am the sixteen year old I would have been had I still been at home.

She always dresses plainly, dark silks with little embroidery, except at the cuffs, and the same rope of pearls around her neck. She always comes to the forest before breakfast, to the secret places where the huntsmen never ride, to fern-filled hollows close to the stream and perhaps to other places I do not yet know. She is kind and beautiful.

And I cannot stop thinking about her.

What am I doing here? One snap of their fingers and I could be back in Lincoln prison. I have darted and dodged in the shadows for many months now and I have been lucky at Bradgate Hall. Nobody has asked where I am from or where I am going.

But these new feelings, the ones I have for Jane, frighten me.

They might make me careless.

There is a place where the water widens and falls frothing over the rocks into a deep pool. Sometimes, when we stop to eat and Thomas falls asleep, or at morning light, I go and read by the water and think of Jane. Then I am truly in heaven.

For the first time in months, I feel my whole body relax. Only the scar on my right palm itches. And, as the evenings grow lighter and longer, I sit outside cleaning my axe with an oily rag, running my fingers along its curved steel, until it shines like the moon. Then I stare at my reflection in the last light. My eyes still hold their wary look.

The priesthood should be your passion, they say, not a Protestant.

Jane

I tiptoed through the great hall. Last night's fire flickered in the grate, giving enough light to cast my shadow on the wall. The oak dresser loomed, its silver plate catching the early morning light.

I was on my way to the forest.

Before I reached the outside door, I stopped to look at a portrait on the wall. It is not a good painting like the one by Hans Holbein, but it is a good likeness, my mother says. The face of my mother's uncle, Henry the Eighth, looked down at me. Except for his beard, it could have been her: broad face, broad lips, broad neck. In my head, I thanked him as I did every day for steering England away from the Catholic Church.

As I put out my hand to open the door, my sister Catherine came clattering down the staircase. She is two years younger than me, and her skin is like cream – not one sunspot dapples its surface. And there is no Tudor red in her hair. It is as brown and gleaming as a new chestnut. Mary clung to her nightdress. Poor little Mary, as twisted as a young willow from the day of her birth.

"Father wants to see you," Catherine said.

"Why?" My heart thudded.

"Perhaps it's something to do with Ned." She giggled and made kissing noises in my face.

"May your tongue split!" I shouted, reaching up to slap her. She stepped back and Mary hid behind her, pulling a face at me.

"Stop this noise!" Ellie had appeared at the kitchen door. "The servants can hear you! Why are you squabbling?"

None of us replied.

Ellie shooed my sisters away. Then she came back to me, frowning. "Why has your father sent for you? I warned you, Jane! Didn't you see me shake my head?"

"Yes, yes, Ellie, I know, but I felt sorry for him. What is the point of saving him if he is to starve and steal again and be hanged a second time?"

She ignored my question. "Don't anger your father. He may let you off lightly."

I would have laughed at her words if my father had not bellowed for me at that moment from the library door.

He was already holding the whip when I went in. I took a sharp breath. My father had often slapped and pinched, but he had never whipped me. People say how alike we look and it is true. His face is also slender and his skin is pale. But his mouth is softer than mine and for that reason he hides it under a long moustache.

My mother was sitting next to him, her lips pressed tight. A ruff hid her neck, the latest fashion from London. Is this how parents greet their daughter when they return home? Any other mother or father would have kissed and petted me and asked me how my lessons went.

I curtsied. "Good day, sir. Good day, madam. Welcome home."

Their faces hardened in the silence. I stared past them at the stag's head on the wall. I had looked at it in death many times: its hacked neck grey with dust; its antlers laced with cobwebs. Here, in this room, the huntsman and its victim are forced to face each other every day.

"Get on with it, Henry!" The anger in my mother's voice astonished me.

My father raised his whip and pulled my right hand towards him. I flinched as my skin split, sprinkling blood onto my cuff – royal blood, the cause of all my troubles.

"I did not expect to return from London and find a newcomer living amongst us!" he snapped. "It is not for you to interfere in estate matters."

To my surprise, my father did not ask where Ned had come from. I wondered what he would say if he knew that he had been dangling from the nearest gallows. In spite of my fear, I enjoyed the thought.

I hesitated. I had to ask, even if he whipped me again. "Will you let him stay, sir?"

He sighed. "Yes, for now, and only because Thomas has asked. But stay away from this boy! He may take advantage of your kindness because you are a woman." I must have smiled because he brought his fist down hard on the table. "You are the most difficult of my daughters, Jane," he said quietly, as if he had said this many times to himself. "We do not like strangers here. How do we know he will not murder us in our beds?"

"How does he know that we shall not murder him in his?" The words spilled out before I could stop them.

My mother leaned forward. She is a large woman, my mother, and her chin doubles as she speaks. Unlike my father, who thinks only that I fear the physical pain, she knows my deepest fear. "Remember, Jane, there are worse punishments than the whip." She paused and glanced at my father. He nodded. "We have been arranging your marriage in London. Then you will learn the meaning of obedience."

Her words made me tremble as she knew they would. Marriage was something that happened to other girls – something far off and frightening, like death. Something I dreaded.

Who would they make me marry? William Parnell, as plain as a garden sparrow? Or one of the Dudley hawks? Dudley was the King's Protector, the devil himself who had spawned five sons. Or…

My father's voice cut across my thoughts. "Dudley thinks you will suit Edward very well."

The *King*? My head was throbbing now, as well as my palm. I had last seen him four years ago, so full of anger as he spoke to his advisors that he had plucked every feather from a falcon, and when I begged him to stop he had torn it apart. No, I could not marry such a man.

The room tilted around me and I put my hand to my neck. Edward was Henry's son and Henry's wives had had a habit of dying. Like father, like son. If Edward could do that to a bird, what would he do to me? I stayed silent, afraid of what I might say.

My mother continued, "And I pray every day that you will become a woman soon. You will only marry when you can bear a child." My cheeks reddened. "Now kneel for your blessing."

As I knelt, the thought came to me: how can the man that blesses me in the name of God marry me to such a man as Edward?

I stumbled from the room. "I shall not marry the King!" I muttered to myself. "I shall not marry anybody. I want to be free to choose my own life."

Somebody caught hold of my arm and placed a finger across my lips. It was Ellie, fear shadowing her face. "Hush!" she whispered. "You know that in this house such words are treason."

Ned

Who am I?

A bright sky encloses me and a sharp wind scents the
air with hawthorn blossom. It is Sunday, my day of
rest, and I have climbed Beacon Hill, knee-deep in
honeysuckles and enchanter's nightshade. Below me lie
river valleys and forests, and at last I see what I have
come for: on the north horizon – faint, but clear –

the spire of Lincoln Cathedral.

Not only do I imagine our house, but I hear my father's voice as he urges me to study: "When Edward dies," he used to say, "and it is rumoured that he will die young, his sister Mary will sit on the throne of England. It will be a glorious day, my son! A Catholic monarch again! Until then we must keep our heads down."

My father aged daily as Protestantism crept up on us like the sea, eroding the old faith like the face of a cliff. Everything, everyone that was dear to him was slowly swept away: his brother, a Catholic priest, gone to exile in France; the old Common Prayer book replaced by a new one encouraging the congregation to take part in the church service, and – the worst thing of all – no longer was the bread and wine thought to transform into Christ's flesh and blood during Mass.

Our daily life became more and more difficult. My father taught Latin and Greek to the choirboys at Lincoln Cathedral, only a stone's throw from our house on the hill below. One day, when I was about ten years old, he was dismissed. The new faith asked for Mass to be sung in English. My father took in private pupils. We sacked all the servants except one and we washed in cold water in winter so that we need not light a fire.

The house fell into disrepair around us, but this was nothing compared to the ruin of our faith.

"Enough is enough!" my father wept one day. And from then on, we attended an illegal Catholic Mass held deep inside such a forest as this, two hours' walk from Lincoln. We would set off at dawn, every Sunday, whatever the weather, with the Proctors, our neighbours. That was the only time I ever thought about the boy king on the throne telling us what we could and could not do. "How can such a young boy have all that power?" I used to ask my father, but he explained patiently that it was the men around him who had all the power.

Dark thoughts fill my mind. At the beginning of last winter, all of us at that Mass were arrested. There was no trial. They took us straight to Lincoln Castle, which then served as the city's prison.

Next to us were three Catholic monks chained to a pillar. We prayed to God all day to save them, but they died of starvation and were thrown into a communal grave without the last rites.

As the days passed, it was not the dirt or the disease or the damp that was the worst thing. It was one of our gaolers. He was a runt of a man with a twitch in his right eye, too skinny to lay a whip or a hand on us. Words were his weapon.

My heart lurches.

He terrified us with stories of a black dog, whose ghost roamed the prison. He said its teeth were as long as a man's arm and as sharp as his razor. He said it would come looking for us at night. Mistress Proctor prayed as her husband lay in the straw like a pig in its own filth, howling and roaring with fear. Sarah Proctor thought only of escaping.

Plump little Sarah Proctor! Who would have thought it? To my shame, I laughed at her. But she had made up her mind. With a nail taken from her shoe, she scratched away the mortar around one of the stones. I watched her, my mind dulled by fear of the black dog. After a week, she begged me to help her as her arms thinned.

We worked together as soon as the last light had gone. I listened for the roaring dog but he never came and I grew braver. During the days, my father sat against the loosened stone, his body weakening with fever.

Sarah took her chance one November night when the guards were drunk and snoring. Everybody helped to lift out the stone, but nobody wanted to go with her – not even her parents. We were all too afraid.

She wriggled through easily, thin enough now.

"Go with her, Ned!" My father's whisper was urgent. "Go to your uncle. It is your chance." I refused.

He groaned. "It makes no difference whether you are here. There is nothing more you can do for me, except pray. I shall live or die whether you are here or not. Go, Ned. *Please!*"

I did not follow Sarah then. But my father was dead by morning and there was no doubt that he had willed it to force me. We propped up his dead body in front of that stone until I left that night. I stood briefly in the empty street, glancing at the rooftops of Lincoln below. Then I went home long enough only to pick up my father's crucifix, his rosary, a Bible and a book written by Plato. I ran towards the city walls overlooking the river where I had swum with my friends on sunlit days.

As I headed south, I kept turning back to glance at the cathedral spire. And on the day I could no longer see it, the bond was broken. Like a child set free from its mother, I quickened my pace.

One more glance at the silhouetted spire and I set off down the hill.

Who am I?

A boy who is falling in love.

And falling in love with a girl who is – if I am not mistaken from the look in her eyes – as much at the mercy of the world as I am.

My life was organized for me into a strict routine: rise at five, prayers, breakfast, lessons, dinner, music lessons, supper, prayers and bed at nine. To the many visitors who came to the house, my life must have seemed happy. But nothing could quell the fear inside me, not even Ellie's herbs. I was trapped – and as I struggled like a bird inside my trap, fear consumed me:

fear of becoming a woman, fear of my parents, fear of the hunt, fear of marrying.

There was little time for leisure, except a short daily walk in the deer park and sometimes to the edge of the forest. Ellie would not go any further. "I know it's silly," she would say, "but I feel as if the dark side of our nature's in there, the part that we all fear."

"She is afraid of the wolves," my tutor, Doctor Aylmer, would tease. "*I* shall take you, Jane."

We went on my last birthday, when I was fourteen, a day of autumn winds and climbing clouds. As we entered the forest, Doctor Aylmer slowed to catch his breath and I walked on, drawn by the beauty of the trees. They huddled close above me, trapping me in a loneliness so deep that I was afraid.

Where was I?

I closed my eyes, but the forest noises still made my heart thud: branches creaking, leaves rustling, birds calling. I forced myself to peep through half-closed eyes. A light filled the forest, soft and shimmering and I looked up, searching for the source, but the sun was not shining. And when I put out my hand, it had no warmth.

Then just as quickly, the light dimmed. But my heart had filled with joy.

I found my way back to Doctor Aylmer easily. "I have seen God," I blurted out, afraid that he would laugh. "I have always believed in Him, but as a child who believes in magic and mystery. Now I truly believe."

He lifted my right hand and kissed it. "We each have to find the light in our own way," he said.

I often went to the forest after that day. And although I never saw the light again, I always felt God there, strong and protecting.

The schoolroom is on the first floor of the right tower, overlooking the walled garden below, and the forest beyond.

It is the warmest and brightest room in the house, full of tables cluttered with books and writing paper, pots of ink and quills. Doctor Aylmer's desk stands on a small platform and in front of him is his pride and joy

– a copy of the first globe made by a German map-maker almost seventy years ago.

Doctor Aylmer never scolded me. Catherine said that he liked me because he and I were both small, but I said it was because I learnt quickly.

One morning, not long after Ned had come to Bradgate Hall, Doctor Aylmer picked up a book lying beside the globe and handed it to me. Its golden title gleamed: *UTOPIA*. I was puzzled. "What does it mean?"

"You are not concentrating," he replied. "Remember the Greek words I have taught you. *Ou* is the Greek for…?"

"For *no*," I replied, "and *topos* means *place*. No place."

"Thomas More, the man who wrote it, means no place that exists on earth – not yet."

"But he was a Catholic!" I protested. "He refused to accept King Henry's divorce. Why should I read a book by a man who was beheaded as a traitor…a man who…?"

I stopped myself, shocked by my anger.

Doctor Aylmer was looking at me, eyebrows raised. "Do not let religion blind you in this way, Jane. This book was written long before those events." His eyes twinkled. "In fact, it was written in the year before your mother was born. 1516."

I laughed. He knew how much I wanted to know my mother's age.

"*Utopia* is a place where women are equal to men." He looked at me carefully. "And where people can believe in whatever religion they choose."

"If it is no place which exists on earth, does that mean heaven?" I asked.

He shook his head and spun the globe. "*Utopia* is an imaginary place – a beautiful island off the coast of the New World...about here. It is what we hope America will be."

I sighed. Knowledge is power, I thought. Doctor Aylmer has taught me that. But in spite of all my learning, the world in which I live is a dark and dangerous one.

"Will I ever go to such a place?" I asked.

He did not reply and the golden letters dimmed in front of me.

Suddenly, I was afraid again.

The stream trickles between the twisted roots of old oaks, narrowing between granite rocks until it widens into a pool.

It is my favourite place.

I went there on the first warm morning of spring, about a week after my beating. I needed its calm. I thought the sky had fallen to the ground where bluebells showed under the trees. They sprang from the blood of Norman soldiers slain in battle, Doctor Aylmer said. Raindrops from last night's storm still clung to them, splashing my velvet shoes, dampening my dress. A long way off, sounds that I hated carried through the trees: hunting hounds baying and hawks squawking as they scanned the sky.

The stream was fast and furious after the rain and I heard the echo of its fall before I reached it. The wind scattered drops of water onto my face and I licked my lips, tasting the wild watercress.

A mist hung over the pool, shafted by sunlight, which reached the rocks and took my eye to the water's edge.

Somebody was bathing there. I stared.

It was Ned.

I had never seen a naked person before, neither man nor woman. I closed my eyes but it was too late. I had already seen Ned's curling body hair and that part of him that made him a man dangling like a winter catkin.

As he climbed from the pool, I caught sight of his back and buttocks. His skin was criss-crossed with raised scars.

Scarred back, scarred hand. What had happened to him?

I waited until Ned had dressed himself before I came out from the trees. He was sitting on the rocks, reading. Now his face looked like an angel's in the pale light, his silver hair curling around a skin that had hardly been roughened by a razor.

I dropped a pebble into the pool and when he glanced up, I straightened my headdress and smoothed my skirts, conscious of his eyes on me.

"What are you doing here?" I asked.

He stood up and bowed. "Jack does not like to see me read."

I looked away then. I did not know what else to say to him. I do not know any boys of my age and my closest male relation in age is the King of England. I heard my mother's voice in my head: *You must only converse with men of royal rank, Jane. To all other men, you give orders.* But it was too late – I had to know what he was reading. So I asked him as he slipped the book into his pocket.

"The body is only the place where our soul is held," he said in Latin. *"The body is a cage and the soul is like a bird inside it, trying to escape and fly home. When the body dies, the soul is released from its prison and goes on living."*

"Plato," I whispered. Tears filled my eyes at the beauty of the words. A desire to tease took hold of me – it would hide my emotion. "Why was he nicknamed Plato?" I asked.

"Because his forehead was big and round like a plate!"

"Who was his best friend?"

"Socrates, with the big bulging eyes!" He laughed as

he spoke. "He was the wisest man in Greece just because he knew that he did not know everything. He loved trees. He walked every day in the oak forests around Athens."

"*My* eyes bulge," I said, although I did not know why.

"No, they are beautiful," he replied.

I turned my head away, biting my lip, confused. I knew that I was plain. My mother's eyes told me every day. She tried hard for her sake, not for mine: the latest ruff from London to hide my scrawny neck, heavy dresses to thicken my body, thick-soled shoes to give me height. *She* had never told me how beautiful my eyes were.

"You look afraid," he said. "I saw it in your eyes that first day."

"Do not say such stupid things." I wish I had not spoken so sharply.

He stood behind me and we looked down at our reflections in the water. "Look! Your forehead is furrowed and your eyes are frightened. Why?"

"My father and mother are always angry with me,"

I replied. "They bellow and bluster like the north wind over every little thing."

"*My* father never raised his voice in anger," he said. "And if I was angry, he always put a hand on my shoulder to quieten me. 'Begin again, Edward,' he used to say. 'Words spoken in anger have no power.'"

"Then you have a wise father," I said, softening my voice. I looked at him, puzzled as I had been that first day.

Who are you? I thought.

Later, I stared at my reflection in my looking glass.

Your eyes are beautiful.

I blushed as I remembered. *Were* they? I leaned forward to look more closely. Did I look any different? Inside, I felt as if my heart was unfreezing, spreading a warmth through my body.

Ned

There are five of us crammed in the cart and Thomas driving the horse: myself, Jack, two gamekeepers – Daniel and Will – and a girl of about my age who giggles and holds a bunch of buttercups under my chin. "Do you like butter?" she asks, and I laugh because it is the thing I missed most on the highway.

Her name is Alice and she is from the next village,

she tells me. Bradgate Hall is the furthest she has ever travelled. She is a new laundry maid. "Her Ladyship wants all the washing out to dry before breakfast." She holds out her hands to me. "Look at my skin, it's split already. I never knew life would be this hard." She looks straight at me. "I want to get married. Get away from all this drudgery."

Her smile deepens, crinkling the corner of her eyes. They are bright blue and they hold me in their gaze. They are not as beautiful as Jane's, but I enjoy pressing against her as the cart jolts, enjoy the scent of soap on her skin.

Jack pulls her roughly towards him.

It is strange to be out on the highway again. The last time I came this way, I was with Jane. I close my eyes as we pass the gallows.

The alehouse is called *The Maid in the Moon* and it stands just beyond the crossroads. It is the first I have entered, although I do not admit it. A girl sets jugs of ale in front of us and the talk begins: of the coming summer, of the King and how he is making life difficult for the woodmen.

"His Lordship wants to cut down some of the wood to make way for cornfields," Thomas begins, "but if he does, he has to leave twelve trees standing in every acre."

Daniel yawns and looks across the table at Jack. Jack thumps the table. "God's teeth, Tom!" he shouts. "I did not come here to talk about trees!" He thumps the table again. "Nay, I did not. What I want to know is this – is our young King saving himself for the Lady Jane?"

"Hush, Jack!" Alice says. "You'll get us all sacked."

Jack glances at me. "Our innocent Lady Jane," he says.

"What do you mean?" They all stop drinking and gape at each other in surprise at the sound of my voice.

Jack grins. "I mean, Master Ned without a family name, that by this time next year, our sweet little Lady Jane'll be the Queen of England." He circles his fingers around his neck, "and she'll chop off all us heads if we don't behave!"

A shiver runs through me and I want to be sick. In the back of my mind, I know that Jane's father will arrange a good marriage for her. That is the custom. I have stopped myself thinking about it. But the King of England!

The thought takes my breath away.

Jack sneers as he grabs my sleeve. "Where have you sprung from, pretty boy? You speak soft like a gentleman. You read when everybody else is at sport. You're more scarred than a fox's face. Who are you? A spy?"

The others, all except Thomas and Alice, pick up their ale and thump the table. "Who are you?" they chant. "Who are you?" Their faces blur in front of me, swaying and sweating. Panic rises in my throat. Jack puts up his fists. "Let's see if we can beat the answer out of you."

They drag me outside. Thomas cannot stop them. I stagger in the dark, but the cold air sobers me, puts me back on my guard.

I do not enjoy fighting, although if I have to do it, I will. My uncle taught me, for my father was too gentle a man and I had never known the rough and tumble of brothers. I was shocked at the time. "But you are a priest!" I protested. "You should turn the other cheek." "I only fight to defend myself, Ned," he replied.

I let him teach me and now I am glad. Because I am fair-skinned and fair-haired, boys who do not know me assume that I cannot fight.

Jack is brimming with anger.

I stand still as my uncle has taught me, watching Jack jump and dance around me, fists in the air, trying to make me go after him and when he finally comes close, I can tell by his heavy breathing that he is already tiring. My first punch catches him on the nose as I intend and he howls with surprise at the sight of blood on his shirt.

He lashes out at my ducking head, so hard that he falls over. It is all over in minutes: Jack squirming on the flagstones and Alice running to see what happened and Daniel telling him it's his own fault and slapping me on the back.

There is little talk on the way back. Alice and Thomas sing, and the others lie asleep at our feet. Birds are still flitting through the trees looking for their last supper, calling to each other before they find a spot to sleep.

I watch a slice of moon behind the trees. If I had known that Jane was to marry the King, would I...? Vomit rises in my throat and I lean over the side of the cart and let it splatter into the wind.

Ned was in my thoughts as soon as I woke up and this alarmed me because I was used to thinking only of God at such times. He had not come to the pool that morning and disappointment made me bad-tempered.

When I came back, Catherine was sitting in my bedchamber window stitching her sampler. "I know something about Ned and Alice," she whispered, watching my face carefully.

"Who is Alice?"

"The new laundry maid."

She took out a ball of thread. I did not ask her what she knew and she was bursting with impatience to tell me. "Alice likes Ned!" she said at last. "But she swims in the stream with Jack."

"Is that all? What a lot of fuss about nothing!" My cheeks burned. "You must not listen to gossip, Cate."

"It's not gossip. Alice told me herself. I've just seen her."

"You should not have been talking about such things with her."

She ignored the disapproving look on my face and asked me if I knew how oranges grew, and when I did not reply she said that the female was pollinated by the male, just like people, but people did not need bees to help them. She stopped to bite off a piece of thread. "Do you not want to be alone with a man, Jane?" she asked. "Do you not want a man to touch you?"

I shook my head. "Your thoughts are wicked!" I moved away from her and sat in the chair at the foot of my bed.

"My thoughts are natural," she replied. "That's what a man and a woman are meant to do."

"Where have you learned such things?"

"My body has taught me. We're not animals, Jane. We're meant to please each other." She giggled. "Do you think Ned has such urges? Alice says that all men do."

Was she taunting me?

My heart tightened. I did not answer, but opened my book. I tried to read but a memory flashed in front of me. Five years ago, my parents had sent me to live with the King's uncle, Thomas Seymour, in London. I was to learn obedience. The King's sister, the Lady Elizabeth, also lived there. One morning, as I was walking past Elizabeth's bedchamber, I had glimpsed Seymour in his nightshirt and slippers, smiling stupidly, his face red. The Lady Elizabeth was jumping on the bed, her breasts bouncing, and he leaned over and pulled her down by her ankles. Then his hand slipped inside her nightgown, tickling and slapping her bare flesh until I had to look away.

Catherine was stitching again as she spoke. "I can't wait to be married. I shall have my own house. I'll have gold everywhere, like this thread. Golden dresses..." She giggled. "...and golden curtains hanging around our marriage bed."

Her stupidity irritated me. "You will not be allowed to have a marriage bed for many years. You are too young for childbearing."

"Spoilsport," she said, pouting. She put her sampler on the cushion and drummed her fingers on the windowpane.

I carried on reading Heinrich Bullinger's book. He is a Protestant reformer living in Zurich and I have been writing to him for the last two years.

"Doctor Bullinger says that parents must keep their daughters from lewd conversation. You should remember that, Cate."

"Do you like Ned?" she carried on. "Alice says that—"

"Leave me alone!" I shouted.

She ran out, slamming the door, and I picked up her sampler and pulled out the golden threads she had sewn. Then I sat in front of my looking glass and lifted my lips with my fingertips to make them smile.

At the edge of the forest where the trees thinned, I heard a cry. At first, I thought it was a bird being hawked and I ran on. Then I realized it was coming from the ground, close to my feet. I looked down.

It was a raven caught in a snare.

He struggled at first, but then lay still as if waiting for death. I knelt beside him, trying to loosen the net, and he flapped his wings, afraid, and in his struggle he pecked the little finger of my right hand. When I held him at last, I saw that he was only a fledging and new to the world.

"Throw him into the air." It was Ned's voice. I turned round to see him standing behind me. "That will force him to fly."

I threw him gently. The raven spread his wings, soaring above us and we laughed out loud as we watched him. As he disappeared from sight, Ned's face darkened. "You did not tell me you were to marry the King of England!"

"Does it matter?" I shivered.

"Yes. I like being with you. I hate the days when I do not see you."

"And I want to be with you," I whispered. "I have never felt like this before."

"And Edward?"

I shook my head. "It is my duty; you know that, Ned. But I do not want to be the Queen of England. They always die, either on the block or in childbed."

"It will not happen to you, Jane." It was the first time he had used my name. "I shall not allow it."

My heart pounded. "I would ask for the sword as Anne Boleyn did. She saw too many people suffer from the axe, twitching and crying out between each blow... They say that the executioner does it deliberately so that the victim can repent of their sins between each blow. How they must suffer!"

He looked at me in horror.

"One day, Ned, my life might hang by a thread. How many blows of the axe will it take to kill me?"

He put his arms around me and stroked my hair. "Death is only a hobgoblin sent to frighten us in the night," he whispered. "If we believe in everlasting life, we should welcome it with open arms. *The body is only the place where our soul is held*. Do not be afraid. I am here."

We did not see the hunters burst through the trees until they had surrounded us. My mother was leading them, her face fierce, her hair wild around her hat. They fell silent one by one.

Ned stepped forward and bowed. "A raven was caught in the net, madam."

"You should have left it there," she snapped. "They are only good for sniffing out dead bodies. Get back to your work!"

"Go!" I whispered. "Or you will be dismissed."

Ned backed away, bowing until he was out of sight. My mother rode over to me and lashed me once with her hunting whip. Then she lashed the ground around my feet, raising a cloud of dust and I had to run backwards and forwards to dodge her whip. Mary began to cry. Catherine looked away.

"We Greys are one of the most important families in England," my mother shouted. "People look to us to set an example of how to behave. I did not raise you to run around the forest giggling with a woodman!"

"Do not tell father, I beg you. *Please.* Ned will lose his job and he has nowhere else to go."

She leaned over towards me and I thought she was going to slap me. I stared back at her, at the spittle on her lips, at the spidery veins on her chin. "I shall not tell your father. But only because Dudley is here."

She turned her horse and led the hunting party across the deer park and I stumbled after them, rubbing my sore arm. The sun was colouring the windowpanes of my bedchamber, licking around its stone sill, and I wished they were flames that would burn my prison to the ground.

❁   ❁   ❁

He was standing in front of the fire in the Great Hall, his back stooped. As my father beckoned me towards him, Dudley straightened and turned round. He seemed so tall that I could hardly see his face above his ruff. His hooded eyes darted up and down my body.

I shivered.

Now he bowed, his eyes level with mine. I did not curtsy as I should. My legs were trembling too much. My mother came forward, took my arm and twirled me around.

"You see, My Lord, she is becoming a young woman at last."

"Yes, she has a glow about her that I did not expect." He put his hand under my chin. "You have a look of love about you, My Lady."

"Only for life, sir," I said.

He walked past me, to my mother. "Has she become a woman yet?" he asked. My mother flushed. "Sir, this is neither the time nor the place..."

"Has she?"

"No, My Lord. She is small for her age."

"She can only marry when she can bear a child."

My cheeks burned as I watched him leave us. How dare they talk about that most private part of me?

"I thank God there are men like Dudley," my father said. "There has been enough talking in the Privy Council. That is the trouble with the world today. Dudley is a man of action."

"Yes, he murdered men in Norfolk because they were protesting about losing their land," I said. "He hunted them in the fields, killed them where they stood. The cornfields of Norfolk are stained with their blood."

My father was in high spirits that evening. I led Catherine and Mary into the banquet and knelt in front of him. He fingered his goblet of wine, his eyes bright. Then he rose to his feet and moved his hand above my head. "In the name of the Father, and of the Son and of the Holy Ghost."

"Amen," Dudley said. The black feather in his cap fluttered as he spoke.

I hardly spoke that evening. Let them see that I

cannot be bartered, I thought. I was uncomfortable. I usually was in the company of men – except Ned. They remind me of the hunt.

"Jane is tired after her studies." My mother excused me, smiling at me until I looked away.

The din of the trumpets drowned Dudley's reply as the servants carried in silver platters: a boar's head, its mouth stuffed with roasted apples; a peacock royal, its cooked flesh sewn inside its own feathered skin, and flocks of birds.

A rush of wings filled the hall. Were the birds coming to life?

It was a skylark.

It had flown through a high window, terrified, and now it circled until it settled on an oak beam where it sang as we ate. I did not eat meat from that day.

I longed for bed.

My life was in my father's hands. I could never forget that. Later, I lay my head on my pillow and begged sleep to release me from the world.

And by dawn, Dudley had gone.

Ned

The bruises on her arm gleam like buttercups. She is like a wounded animal and I cannot bear the thought. But she has dared to come to the pool and I am glad for that.

"I am sorry, Jane. *Mea culpa.* It is my fault. I should not have spoken to you. But how could she do it! Does she treat your sisters like that?"

"No. Catherine is pretty and knows how to please. And Mary, you saw her... My mother thinks it was because she saw a raven just before her birth."

"You should not have come here. It is dangerous for you."

"My parents have gone to visit my mother's cousin, the Lady Mary." She shudders. "The Catholic Mary. If the King dies, she will be Queen. She will restore England to the old faith."

"How will you bear that?"

"I shall have to, because she is the rightful Queen and it is everybody's duty to follow the faith of their ruler, at least in public, and especially a royal family like mine."

"There are plenty who do not," I reply.

"We shall be drinking Christ's blood in clouds of incense, surrounded by chanting priests and gilded statues." Her voice becomes mocking. "The mystery of faith will come upon the common people again. They will not listen to the Latin Mass. They will perch on their pews like birds longing to be outside." I pull back, revolted by her words, but she cannot stop. "They will no longer understand their faith, Ned, and that is the worst thing of all."

"Well, you must hope that the King lives a long life. Then you can both bring Protestantism to its peak of perfection." I try to keep the bitterness from my voice.

She gasps. "Oh, Ned, it is such a muddle. I do not want to marry the King. I do not even want to marry." She grasps my arm and pulls me. "Let us walk. It will be safe. Charnwood Forest is so big that a bird can hop from tree to tree for six miles."

"I cannot be long. Thomas will be waiting for me as soon as he has eaten."

As we walk, I want to hold her hand, but I cannot. She is running ahead, laughing and spinning around. "We are nearer to God in a forest than anywhere else, Ned! I do not need priests to tell me what to think – at least, not priests dressed from top to toe in gold and silver, telling me what God means and filling my nose with incense. *This* is all I need." She stops and smiles up at me. "Give me the new faith any day. It suits me."

I want her to stop talking. I have seen how religion divides people and already I know that I do not want it to divide her from me.

"What do you want to do with your life, Jane?"

She stands still, surprised. "Nobody has ever asked me that before."

"Tell me!" I insist. "You must know."

"I want to do whatever I choose!" she replies, her face serious. "I want to live where brightly coloured birds fly amongst trees that do not lose their leaves! I want to go to Zurich to talk to the Protestant reformers!" She giggles. "I want to go to Utopia!"

"It seems a grim place. I should not like it."

"You have read it?" she asks.

"Yes. You need not look so surprised."

Her cheeks redden. "Why do you not like it?"

"Nobody is allowed to own their own house and nobody is ever allowed to be idle. There would not be time for walks such as these."

"Oh!" Her voice is flat with disappointment. "I have not read as far as that."

"Have you read the chapter about thieves? Is that why you saved me that day?"

"No. I saved you because it is wrong for one human being to kill another." She hesitates. "Why did you come with me?"

"I had nowhere else to go, but I stayed because I love you." She gasps and I want to hold her close enough to count the sunspots on her face.

A flickering shadow catches my eye and I look up. It is the fledgling raven, smooth beaked and as black as midnight, his feathers faintly gleaming. Beneath him is a rowan bush drooping with berries. The raven leans forward and dangles upside down to pluck them with his beak. He does not wait for them to fall to the ground as some birds do.

We laugh. Then I raise Jane's hand to my lips and kiss it and she does not try to stop me. "Do you love me?"

"I do not know. Do not be angry, Ned. I think with my head, not my heart. It is better that way, and safer. And even if I did, how could *we* ever be together?"

"It is possible to change your life," I say.

She shakes her head. "It is too late for me. Parents draw the map of life for us and it is not a rough draft that can be rubbed out and done again." She keeps hold of my hand. "I have lived the life of a princess since the day I was born, Ned. I have worn the finest silks in summer and the warmest velvets in winter; I have always slept on a goose-feather mattress. But it did not bring me what I wanted. I am still trapped."

I want to tell her who I am.

But I cannot because I like holding her.

For Mary's birth day, we went to Leicester to buy her a new skylark.

We travelled the five miles in a horse-drawn litter. Ours was a handsome cart with a silk canopy. I would rather have ridden one of the horses with Ellie because I do not like being close to my mother or to Mary. I could not bear to be close to her bent back.

So I sat next to Catherine.

The sides of the litter were rolled up for it was a fine day. As the litter swayed, I settled against her plump body and closed my eyes.

What would it be like to be next to Ned? I imagined his hand finding its way to my breasts. I opened my eyes and fanned myself and everybody looked at me, curious.

As we slowed down to pass over a rut, a woman curtsied to us. She carried a small boy on her hip who cried as the dust gritted his eyes. His mother leaned towards him and I held my breath, waiting for her to slap him. But she kissed the top of his head, then blew gently across his eyes until he stopped crying.

I turned my head away. I could not bear the look of love that passed between them. My mother noticed, too, because her eyes moistened. I watched her with new interest. For the first time, I wondered what her dreams were or had been. Had *she* been forced to marry? Had she been disappointed each time she had produced a daughter?

She *had* protected Ned that day, the day when we had set the raven free.

I tried to think of something to say to her, but I could not – and the moment passed.

We rumbled over the river bridge into Leicester town, making our way to the market at Gallow Tree Gate.

It horrified me. Not for its noise and stench, but for the skylarks confined in their cages. *Alauda.* Heavenly stars. The one that Mary chose perched silent and thinly feathered. I shifted from foot to foot, anger rising.

No bird ever sings when it is suffering. That is what Socrates said.

As Ellie pulled out her purse, I knelt and opened the doors of its cage and, with a flap of its wings, it flew out, circling and shadowing the street below. Then it spiralled, soaring and singing until it was out of sight.

"You've killed it!" Mary cried. "It will not know how to defend itself from the big birds."

I had not thought of that.

Although we bought another skylark, nobody spoke

to me on the way home. And if I am honest, I am ashamed of what I did to Mary that day and I do not think that she ever forgave me.

How could I have done it?

They made me hunt. It was my punishment.

I allowed Ellie to dress me. I allowed myself to be sat upon a horse. I allowed myself to be led to the awakening forest where a late frost had come during the night, curling the new leaves.

Hunters surrounded me. Why do they have to make the forest so ugly, so full of death?

"Why should living flesh be ripped apart?" I cried.

"That is the law of the forest," my mother replied. "The strong feed on the weak."

"And the law of life, too!" I said.

Her eyes softened for a moment. "There is no finer sight than the hunt."

"I do not need your cruel world! I have a better one."

"And what world is that, Jane?"

"The one between myself and God. It is far more beautiful than yours."

She ignored me. "The King likes hunting. If you are to be his Queen, you need to learn."

I turned my horse round. "I want no more of this!" My mother tried to rein me in, but I was too fast for her. I rode back the way I had come. The trees around me rustled and horses came from everywhere, hooves pounding, their breath clouding the air.

My father was riding straight at me. "You are going the wrong way, daughter," he bellowed.

"No!" I cried. "My path is the right one, away from this bloody sport."

He reined me in. "This is the sport of kings and soon you will be married to one." He nodded to his men.

They lifted me from my horse and sat me in front of my father, looping one of his reins around my waist. Then he whipped his horse and rode.

Something moved in the trees and I heard the swish of crossbows. This is what I hate about hunting. Death is silent and unseen. A deer staggered in the trees and fell without a sound. At the same time, two hawks circled above it, swooping, rising, swooping again to pluck some poor creature from below. The smell of blood filled the forest. Everywhere I looked, the frost was spotted red.

I beat my fists against my father's cloak. "No more! I beg you, sir, no more!"

He laughed and rode over to the deer, which now lay headless and prickly with arrows. My father leaned over to take the head. As it swung towards me, I was staring into its gentle eyes, watching its twitching mouth, its bleeding neck.

My father dipped his hand into the head and drew it out bright and bloodied. I did not have time to close my screaming mouth. As he smeared my cheeks, I tasted its blood.

Then I fainted.

Ned

My footsteps are light and happy as I make my way home from work that evening. Bright rays of sun show me the way and the birdsong almost deafens me.

At the end of the walled garden is a patch of grass. Already its green is pale with dew. Doctor Aylmer is kneeling there. I hang back, thinking he might be the sort of man who prays as the sun is setting, but I soon see that he is packing away a set of wooden bowls. He beckons me over. I hesitate. I do not know him. I have only seen him preaching in chapel and then only in profile because I sit close to the door.

"Good evening, Ned. How was your work today?"

I give a short bow, surprised that he even knows my name. "Good, thank you, sir."

"You do not see bowls very often since our good King Henry decided to ban them from all but the rich. He thought the ordinary man should be working, not playing." He picks up a small white ball and rolls it in his hand. Then he hands it to me. "Put it in on the grass." I do as he asks and go back to stand by him. "Now take a bowl."

I choose one and, before Doctor Aylmer can speak, I toss it towards the white ball. It flies wide and lands in the flower bed. He laughs, leans forward and gently releases a bowl. It rolls. Then it curves towards the white ball, stopping within a few feet.

He hands me another bowl. "I always think of the white ball as God, Ned. He just sits there all alone and the rest of us have to find a way to reach him. We are the bowls, biased by what our parents have taught us. We fight each other to get to him, knocking each other out of the way in our desperation. Try again."

I release the bowl. It curves and settles between Doctor Aylmer's bowl and the white ball.

"A perfect solution!" he shouts. "You have kept me in the game, but you are closer. A true act of compromise. Well done, Master Kyme." He stares straight into my eyes until my cheeks redden. "I have many friends in Lincoln," he finishes.

Kyme. A Catholic name.

"And have I friends *here*?" I ask.

"Yes, Ned. None of this will pass my lips, unless you want it to."

"I am sick of it all, Doctor Aylmer. You know that my uncle was married to Anne Askew. She took up the new faith and was burned for it because she went too far for the times."

He tugs his ear. "We do not know how this game of religion will end, Ned. *We* make up the rules. *We* put on the right clothes to play. *We* punish others for breaking the rules. Yes, it is a game of great skill."

I sit down on the grass and he looks down at my hands clasped across my chest. "I know how your hand came to be burned, Ned, but next time you may not escape the flames so lightly." He hesitates. "And I have seen the way you look at Jane. You should tell her. Secrets are always dangerous."

"Tell her what? That I have been brought up to be a Catholic priest."

"That you are a Catholic. You are not a priest yet."

"She did not tell me that she was going to marry the King."

"Jane has been brought up and educated to marry well, just as you have been brought up for the priesthood. You are both trapped." He sighs. "She has not experienced the world as you have, Ned. She has learned all she knows from books. She still sees everything in black and white."

"I shall *not* let God keep me from her!"

"Then tell her."

"I do not want to lose her."

He touches my arm briefly. "She is not yours to lose, Ned."

Above us, the sky darkens and the air is as still as it always is in those minutes before the sun slips below the horizon. The clock on the house chimes and Doctor Aylmer turns to go.

I stumble after him. The sun flashes brightly for a second. Then I am plunged into night.

Now I thought about Ned all the time: how kind he was; how green his eyes were; how my heartbeat quickened when he put his arms around me. Sometimes I had to close my eyes to shut out the disapproving faces of my parents. Social rank. England reeked with it. Every gesture, every word, every item of clothing was designed to demonstrate it. I was a princess, groomed to meet princes and kings. I was steeped in the blue blood of royalty.

I threw off these thoughts. Doctor Aylmer had taught me that all men are created equal. And Ned had captivated my mind as well as my heart. Happiness gripped me and made me breathless.

In the evenings, I stayed at the window hoping to see him return from the forest. If I stood on tiptoe, I could see the gate from the park to the walled garden. From there, he would come to the bakehouse.

One evening, Ellie brought Doctor Aylmer to my bedchamber.

"See for yourself, John!" she grumbled.

"She is only looking out of the window, Mistress Ellen. There is a fine view of the forest."

Ellie clucked her tongue. "The forest! That's your fault."

He laughed. *"My fault?"*

"Yes. She can see God in the chapel."

"Still afraid of the wolves, Mistress Ellen?"

I heard her take in a deep breath. "There's only one

wolf out there, and he's in sheep's clothing."

I listened to them, their words bouncing to and fro like a ball. They sounded like my parents. I turned round and glared at them. "That is enough! Ellie!" I said. "If you have something to say, let us hear it now."

"Well…I…I want to…"

Doctor Aylmer cut in. "She wants to know if you have feelings for Ned?"

"Yes."

"That is to be expected," he said. "You saved him from a dreadful death. He will always have a special place in your heart. But…" My body tensed. "You know nothing about him, Jane," he finished.

"I do not care where he has come from or where he is going, Doctor Aylmer. I trust him."

"And what about his hand?" Ellie asked. "Why doesn't he talk about it? There's something strange about his scar. When I took him my comfrey ointment, he wouldn't let me see. He just took the pot and thanked me."

I did not reply. She tried again, but this time she touched a raw nerve. "Ask him how he prays to his God."

"Why should I?"

"He always sits by the chapel door with his eyes closed, that's why."

I looked at Doctor Aylmer for support. "He is passionate about prayer. That is good, is it not?"

He nodded.

My skin prickled and I looked out of the window. Ned was passing through the gate. I would have called to him if Ellie had not reminded me: my parents might be away, but over two hundred people live and work at Bradgate Hall, most of whom would think nothing of tittle-tattling to my parents in the hope of finding future favour with them.

I took hold of Ellie's hands and danced around my bedchamber with her. "Oh, Ellie, I feel as light as a bird! I am so happy!"

Doctor Aylmer chuckled. But Ellie frowned. "Remember, where flowers blossom, so do weeds," she said. "This will only end in tears."

"Let it!" I cried. "But for now, I am happy."

But the shadows fell when I was alone.

I watched the sun slip away. Ellie was right. She usually was. I could have asked him. I *should* have asked him. But in truth, I did not want to hear his answer.

Love made me happy.

I did not realize at the time how much I was changing. Ellie told me later that everybody had noticed. My face glowed, I knew. I tried to hide it in my father's presence for his eyes rested on me as if to say, "Yes, she is no great beauty but she is becoming a woman." Ellie said he was pleased because everyone could see that his oldest daughter was ripe for marriage.

Ned never mentioned the King again. We met by the pool whenever we could. We no longer talked about the King, or the old faith or the new faith. We watched the sun rise and sometimes watched it set. Sometimes, we just watched each other, as if we were caught in a single ray of light. We made up rhymes and riddles. We were in heaven on earth, until a hunting horn or the shriek of a raven roused us.

There were other times when we saw each other in public and each Sunday in the chapel. Although I sat in the family pew at the front, my body told me when Ned was there – a tingling across my skin, a trembling in my heart – and I would glance over my shoulder to find his eyes on me. Catherine noticed because she nudged me and giggled and I wondered if she thought Ned was looking at her.

If *her* eyes lingered on him too long, I saw him with fresh eyes – broad-shouldered from chopping, face the colour of honey, green eyes flecked with brown.

When I glimpsed him from the window of my bedchamber, I knew that he had seen me watching him by the way he swung his axe and put a spring in his step.

"I have been watching for you all day," I would confess when I was with him.

"And I you," he would reply.

"Do you wish I was not a princess?"

"Do you wish I was not a woodman?"

Then we would fall silent.

Ned

I have not spoken to Jane for a week.

I kick the oven hard. "Who is he?" I ask Alice. I am soaked to the skin, drying myself in the bakehouse.

"A student from Germany, Jack says. He's going to study at Oxford after the summer. He speaks to Lady Jane in a language I ain't ever heard. He's a nice young man."

Jealousy shoots through me, hotter than the oven. *Germany.* The hotbed of Protestantism. No wonder she has no time for me. I kick the oven again.

"What do you and Lady Jane talk about in the forest, then?" Alice asks. "Heaven help you if her father finds out." She leans towards me, whispering, "They say he—" She screams. Jack is suddenly there, swinging two dead mice in front of her face, caught from the kitchen traps.

He glares at me. I leave them and as I hurry away, I hear the sound of lips kissing skin.

The days become fiery. At night, when the sky pales instead of darkening, birds cast their shadows against its golden streaks.

Jane's parents have planned a farewell celebration for their visitor. No expense has been spared. I gaze across the deer park dotted with garlanded canopies and flags. In the distance, archery boards turn their faces to the sun. Acrobats somersault across the stream and fire-eaters flame the already hot air.

I am helping to hand out the wine. Jane is sitting next to John Ulmis, flushing with excitement. "I have read everything Doctor Bullinger has written," she is saying: "'*As the sun shines in heaven but is still present on earth with its light and heat, so Christ sits in heaven and is still present on earth in the hearts of all true believers.*' I know I shall never meet him, never hear him preach, but his letters have made my life bearable."

I cough loudly but they do not notice me and I sip wine from each of the goblets in front of me.

"He is the most devout man I have ever met," John Ulmis replies. "His house in Zurich is always open to those in need. He and his wife give money, food and clothing to the poor. Many Protestants in exile find their way to his door and they are never turned away." His voice is light, like a child's, and his words accented like a person who usually speaks German.

He lifts a strawberry and she takes it from him with her mouth, spattering red juice onto her neck, and little Mary claps. Mistress Ellen hands her a spoon.

As I walk on to Doctor Aylmer, jealous feelings,

which I do not like and am not used to, rage inside me.

"You have not told her yet?" he whispers.

I shake my head.

"Do it soon, Ned. And stop drinking! Your face is already flushed."

Dusk comes at last, dampening our skin with its dew. Flaming torches edge the grass. Catherine wheels spin on the trees and I watch their glitter until I grow dizzy and have to look away. People sprawl everywhere, singing, drinking and laughing.

Jane has drunk wine, too. I watch her lean towards John Ulmis. "I pass my days in this earthly prison as if I were dead," she shouts, "while you and Doctor Bullinger and all the other reformers live!"

Has she forgotten me already?

Her father catches hold of her arm across the table, digging his fingers into her flesh. "You have grown wilder these last weeks," he roars. He lets her go and laughs. "It is time she was married, is it not, Master Ulmis? A husband will tame her. Jane is destined for the King! What do you think of that?"

Yes, I shall tell her tonight, while wine loosens both our tongues.

A cartwheel stuffed with straw sits at the top of a slope above the park. A symbol of the sun, Thomas tells me. Lady Jane will light the straw and we will push the wheel. If the flames are still burning when it reaches the bottom of the slope, it will be a fine harvest. If they have burned out, it will be a poor one.

Jack is watching with Alice and Daniel and Will. Opposite us stand Jane and her sisters. She smiles at me as Thomas hands her the flaming torch. The hay flares and we all let go. The wheel gathers speed, showering sparks into the darkening sky. Suddenly, Jack lets out a deafening cry, "Burn! Burn! Catholic, burn!" Thomas warns them to stop, but the others take up the cry, even Alice. "Burn! Burn! Catholic, burn!" They are all baying for blood as they run behind the wheel, prodding the hay with sticks, laughing and screaming their insults.

Jane orders them to stop and I look at her, grateful; but for a moment, as the flames reflect in her eyes, I see a look of delight pass across her face.

Alice screams. The flames have caught her skirt. Jack throws ale over her and she jumps to her feet laughing. I see her later, dancing, her face still blackened by the smoke and I wonder how she can laugh so easily after being licked by the flames of death.

I long for quiet. I make my way to the walled garden. Moths whirr around me as I walk, whitening the air. Jane is sitting by the fountain, silhouetted against the sky, birds roosting in the trees around her.

When she calls to me, my anger spills out, strengthening my voice. "Does Master Ulmis tell you that he reports everything back to Bullinger? Oh yes! They flatter you because they hope that you'll marry the King." I do not know what I am saying. I do not even know if it is the truth, but I have to say it. I have to punish her. "Then they'll have influence over him through you. What better way to benefit their Protestant cause?"

The birds fly in fright from the tree and their shadows flit across her face. "No!" she cries. "That is not true! He writes to me because he wishes to instruct me. He thinks that my mind is worth improving."

To my shame, I throw back my head and laugh. "*You* are his way to the King of England. Why else would he waste his time with you? Ask him! I *dare* you!"

She is crying as she runs from me. And the sun cools for me long before the end of that day.

I did not mean to forget about Ned. I do not take to
people easily. I usually keep myself aloof because I
have worked out that life is simpler that way. I could
not forgive him for what he had said. His words had
hurt me far more than the whip because they had sown
the seeds of doubt in my mind.

Should I ask Doctor Bullinger if it was true? Of all

men, he must respect my female body.

For the first time in my life, I did not know what to do.

"He was jealous, that is all," Ellie said. "For all your learning, you are such an innocent child."

I stayed away from the forest. My head ached and I sat by the window of the summer parlour. The oak trees in front of the house were bursting with life. I watched the raven leaning into the wind, his feathers ruffling, soaring over the treetops. Then he swooped to feed, hiding behind the leaves to peck out insects until he was fat and full.

There is light and shadow in life as there is in the forest, I thought.

I finished reading *Utopia*. I learned of rich landowners who had put hedges and fences around the common land so that the poor people could no longer graze their cattle there or grow crops. Men were forced to live by begging or stealing and when they were hanged for it, their wives and children starved under the very hedgerows that had forced them into poverty.

"Your head is aching because you wear too many

pearls in your hair," Doctor Aylmer said.

"I only have a few," I replied.

"You do not need any at all. God has given you beautiful hair." He picked up his Bible and opened it at a well-worn page. "The Gospel according to St. Peter," he said. "Book Three. Verse Twenty-two. *'Your beauty should not come from outward adornment such as braided hair and the wearing of gold jewellery and fine clothes,'*" he read. "*'Instead it should be that of your inner self, the duty of a gentle and quiet spirit, which is of great worth in God's sight.'*" His voice brightened. "Why do you not ask Doctor Bullinger's advice?"

I understood his rebuke. I had not written to him since Midsummer Day. The seeds had taken root. And, at the same time, I became awkward in John Ulmis's company and I was glad when he left for Oxford at the beginning of August.

I went no further than the walled garden. One morning, I returned through the laundry yard. Alice had put out the ruffs to dry. They perched stiff and headless on their wooden poles. She came to the doorway, her face disappointed when she saw me. As she curtsied, a linen petticoat fluttered on the washing rope and Alice stifled a giggle. I lifted it. Jack stood there. Everything about him was dirty: his hair, his skin, his teeth, his clothes. He was as dirty as Ned had been at the gallows, but Jack did not speak Latin in a gentleman's voice. I was ashamed of my thoughts, and shame made my voice shrill like a child's.

"Why are you not working, Jack?" I asked. "I shall tell my father."

He bowed. "I *am* working, my lady. I have come to collect the dead mice from the kitchen traps."

"That is a pity."

He smiled at Alice and walked away. Her eyes never left him.

I hate Jack. He sets the bird snares. He shoots the forest creatures. He has blood on his hands.

"Take down that petticoat and wash it again," I said. I heard my mother's voice in mine as I spoke.

Do not let him snare you, Alice.

Ned

I pray that she will come to me, since I cannot go to her.

Sometimes I sit by the stream for so long that Thomas scolds me and threatens to find another woodman. Sometimes, on my day of rest, I wait from dawn until dusk on Beacon Hill.

August brings days and nights so sultry that I cannot sleep above the bakehouse. So I sleep on the hill, watching the moon. People say that it is dangerous to sleep in the moonlight. It will make you blind. But it is not that thought that keeps my eyes open. It is the beauty of the moon. Its craters and crevices like the face of an old friend.

One morning, as I scramble down the hill, I shiver and look up. Jane is coming towards me, the pearls in her headdress gleaming. She tramples the dying foxgloves in her haste. She does not even glance at the rising sun. I run towards her, catching her around the waist so fast that she stumbles and we start to roll down the hill. She stiffens and clings to me.

"Let yourself go limp," I whisper.

We roll on as if for ever, laughing, until we stop with a jolt that takes away our breath. Her hair has escaped and it hides her face.

"I am sorry," she begins. "I should not have…"

I am holding her before she finishes, stroking her hair and asking her to forgive me.

Jane

The best days of my life began. The sun blazed every day and a dry dust coated the countryside. The corn grew taller than me and when the breeze bowed its ripening heads, they showed rosy poppies.

We met under the rock by the stream, talking in its cool green, dangling our feet in the water.

Ned kissed my hand. "Come away with me, Jane.

I can take you to the life you want. To Zurich. To Heinrich Bullinger. Wherever you wish."

"Oh, Ned, I cannot imagine such a life! How would we live?"

He ignored my question. "We would be together, that is all that matters. We could live a life of Christian perfection. Let me take you." His voice became urgent. "Come with me, Jane. *Please*."

I sighed. "Whatever I do, my father will have me hunted down. It would never be possible."

As I walked home, I sometimes imagined that Ned was really a prince sent to live in the forest by his family to test me, like beauty and the beast...and my father would give his blessing, and...

Then I stopped and laughed at myself. Ned was no beast – and I was certainly no beauty.

One Sunday, the chapel was heady with the scent of lilies and boughs of lavender. It intoxicated me more than the communion wine. My blood flowed warm. I felt truly alive.

Harvest dust filled the air, greying the sun, and already the ravens were squabbling over the stubble in the fields. I wanted the cool green of the forest.

The path I followed was deep with bracken and ferns and cow parsley. Dragonflies buzzed low, hovering for insects.

The sound of laughter stopped me. Then the rustle of petticoats. I stopped and listened, listened to the sound that skin makes when it comes together. I wanted to know. I peeped through the cow parsley. I could see very little, only that Alice and Jack were lying together as one person, grunting and gasping, their skins gleaming.

So this is what men and women do.

I crept away. And when I reached the path again, I ran, remembering Ned's skin against mine when we had rolled down Beacon Hill, growing warm at the thought.

Ned taught me to swim. He turned his back as I shed my clothes down to my silk shift, and went into the water. He held my hands as I kicked, and promised not to let me go. Then, when I was tired, he took me to the bank and I stood on the stones, shaking off the water. Did he peep as I put on my dress?

Alice swims in the stream with Jack. That is what my sister had sneered. I should not have done it. Ned sensed that I was unhappy.

"It is not wrong to have fun, Jane. I used to swim with my friends in the river. It was part of summer."

"But you were not a princess!" I said.

He was not angry.

"And there is gossip about Jack and Alice. What if somebody sees us as they saw them?"

"Nobody saw them," he said. "Jack boasted about it whenever he could. I shall not."

We sat and watched the squirrels darting up the tree trunks, searching for acorns, and glimpsed wood mice scuttling through the leaves. The birds were silent because Thomas was already at work. Ned picked up his axe. "The oak trees once complained to the gods that as soon as they grew tall, the axe chopped off their heads. The gods laughed and said that they had no right to complain since they had produced the wood for the handle."

I met Mary long before I reached the edge of the forest. Her eyes gleamed with satisfaction as she tried to run from me. I ran after her, caught her and shook her hard.

"You deformed demon!" I cried. "If you say one word...to anybody...if ever I am Queen, I shall..." I put my hands around her neck. "I shall chop off your head."

A taste of winter came suddenly for the harvest thanksgiving, whitening the newly ploughed soil. The smell of wet earth clinging to the roots of cabbages and carrots, mingled with the sharp scent of apples, pears and plums. A huge loaf of milk-glazed bread decorated the altar. If it turned into Christ's body – as the Catholic Church believed – he would be a giant.

A flash of gold brought the wine chalice closer. What if the wine I am about to drink really is Christ's blood?

I cannot drink blood. That is the act of a cannibal.

My mother dug her elbows into my ribs and I let the wine smear my lips.

Ned

The scorching sun cools to the shifting colours of autumn and they glint red-gold like Jane's hair.

When the wind blows cold and the hunt begins, Jane takes me further into the forest where it is dark and wild. It is the deepest part of Charnwood where even the hunt does not go because the undergrowth is too dense. I look up at the trees with an experienced eye: elms, larches, spruces, all so crowded that no light reaches the ground. Dank smells rise from the forest floor.

It is desolate.

We come to a roofless ruin, its walls held together by ivy and bindweed. "This is Ulverscroft Priory," Jane tells me. "The last prioress to live here was called Agnes. She ran away to marry the man she loved and came here when he died. As you can see, it was destroyed. The new faith does not need such places," she finished.

I swallow my anger. I knew that it had happened everywhere in England – it had happened in Lincoln: Henry the Eighth closed down all the monasteries and priories as he turned away from the Roman Catholic faith. Monks and nuns became beggars at the roadside.

Inside the ruins, there are remains of tiles on the floor and in a wooden chest a hooded grey cloak and silver candlesticks still holding their candles. I tie branches to make a roof and nail back the hanging door and block up the window gaps with stones.

We light the candles. Jane leans against me and we make shadow shapes on the wall with our hands: a bird, a butterfly, a scurrying cloud. Then she picks up the candle and watches the flames flicker.

I lean towards her, whispering, "Plato says that the shadows in the cave are…" But Jane is not listening. A look of delight passes across her face, like the midsummer night when she lit the wheel on the hill, when Jack shouted…

I snatch the candle from her.

"They burnt some poor fool once, in Leicester," she is murmuring. "He smacked too much of the old faith. They said his friend was allowed to hang gunpowder around his neck, to hasten his death. But it was damp. Then his family piled on more faggots, but they were also damp. It had been a wet spring. So he burnt slowly."

My voice shakes. "It is barbaric. You have never talked of such things before. You cannot bear to see even a butterfly die. Where do these thoughts come from?"

"A butterfly is different, Ned. It can do no wrong."

"And *me*? Did I deserve to hang that day? You did not stop to ask!"

"They were not burning you. I knew it had nothing to do with your faith."

I put my fingers across her lips. "Do not talk of such things."

She falls silent and relaxes against me. And when the candles gut, it is time to leave. We walk together to the foot of Beacon Hill. Then we go our separate ways.

The mists thicken every day, damp and smoke scented. And this darkness takes us deeper into ourselves.

This is our world.

Jane likes to run her fingers along my good hand, until one day she strokes the scarred one. "Why did you leave your home?"

I toss back my hair. "I have no answers! I am in a muddle and I do not know what I want. It suits me very well to be here. That is all I can tell you."

"What happened to your hand?"

I do not answer and she does not ask me again. "My

head is always in a muddle, too," she says. "That is the nature of youth, Ellie says. She says she would not wish to be young again for all the honey in the beehive." She sighs. "I wish I were like Catherine. She is only two years younger than me and already she knows her place in the world."

She tells me that she will go to London for Christmastide. Jealousy stabs my heart.

"Will the King be there?" I ask.

"Yes," Jane replies. "Usually he moves to Greenwich Palace for the festivities, but he is too unwell to travel." She glances at me. "And too unwell to marry me."

We walk back arm in arm to the edge of the forest, slowly, lingeringly, not wanting our time together to end.

Jane

Imagine every castle you have ever heard about in fairy tales. Turrets and towers and battlements that reach for the sky, gilded and gaudy with painted animals. Walls with chequered squares of chalk and stones like a great chessboard.

This was Whitehall Palace.

King Edward's winter home and his seat of

government. Conceived by his father, King Henry. Here he and Anne Boleyn had dreamed of a son. Here Anne Boleyn had been arrested and taken to the Tower.

I had never seen it at Christmastide. It rose by the River Thames, frosted by a light snow, sparkling in the flaming torchlight.

The ceiling of my bedchamber was sky blue and golden. It soothed me like the forest. Beautiful objects lay everywhere: medals and maps; boxes, some of painted leather, some of carved ivory layered with cool pearls; tortoiseshell combs and diamond-studded brushes.

The city of London rose in the distance, silhouetted against the winter's lemon light. I glimpsed the outline of church spires and the high steeple of St. Paul's Cathedral. That night, I lay listening to the sounds of the river for a long time: oars creaking, ferrymen calling. And the splashing of the water made me think of Ned by the stream.

There must have been at least three hundred of us in the Great Hall that Christmastide Eve. Suddenly, silence fell and everybody turned towards the gallery. A thin boy stood there, wearing a doublet of blue velvet.

King Edward.

My eyes were drawn to his hands gripping the edge of the balcony – long and white and tapering like candles. Men on either side held him upright.

I was so shocked by his frail body and his gaunt face that I forgot to curtsy. I stood gaping.

"Curtsy to your King." It was Dudley, nudging me sharply from behind.

"It is not for you to tell me what to do," I whispered. "It is for the King."

Dudley leaned over me. I could feel his breath on my neck. "Do not forget that *I* tell the King what to do."

I was right to dread Dudley.

When the King had left, I stood in a corner with Catherine and Ellie. Dudley's head stood out above the others. Each time his eyes rested on mine, I looked away. At last, he strode over to us with his five sons. Guildford, the youngest, was a tall boy with cheeks as flushed and as fleshy as a robin's breast. Only his lips were bloodless. He bowed so low to Mary that his hat fell at her feet. She picked it up and handed it back. Catherine and I laughed out loud. We could not stop ourselves. Then he stepped back in line with his brothers and walked on.

"I detest them all," I whispered to Catherine. "If they come near me again, I shall go to my bed."

"They are not to blame for what their father does any more than we are to blame for what our father does," she replied.

Touché? My sister was becoming wise at last.

She was exquisite that evening. Her dress was blue to match her eyes and edged with silver fur. Silk threads lit up her hair. Except for my pearls, I wore no jewellery with my sombre dress. I did not want to attract attention.

John Dudley's voice reached my ears. "I taught them a fine lesson," he was boasting. "The men of Norfolk have not caused me any trouble since that day." I paused to listen. "They say that their leader's body is still hanging at Norwich Castle." He laughed. "Yes, Ket's skeleton is a sober reminder to the good people of Norfolk!"

I pushed myself into the centre of his circle. "Have you read your Bible, sir?" I asked. "We are told in Proverbs that if you oppress the poor, you insult the God who made them. But kindness shown to the poor is an act of worship."

John Dudley looked down at me. Amusement lightened his voice. "The Bible also says that wicked people bring about their own downfall by their evil deeds. They were traitors, and in this country we kill them." He turned back to his sons as if he did not expect a reply.

"They were just poor people looking for an honest living," I said. "The traitors were the rich landowners who took the common land from them. What did you expect them to do?"

John Dudley sniffed the air as if scenting a fox and his sons laughed, Guildford the loudest of them all. Then he sighed. "God punishes his enemies. Have you not read Isaiah? *'Their corpses will not be buried, but will lie there rotting and stinking.'*"

I stood straight, trying to make myself look taller. "They were not your enemies," I replied. "And if you had read Isaiah properly, you will know what else was written: *'Do not use your power to cheat the poor.'*" I heard only the sound of my own voice. "And everywhere in the Bible we are told to love one another. Tell me, sir, does the King do *everything* you tell him?"

John Dudley gasped, angry, but his face relaxed as my father reached me. Dudley nodded to the musicians in the gallery. "She preaches well, sir," he said to my father. "We should put her in the pulpit tomorrow. Then we can all sleep off our wine!"

He laughed and I hated him. But I had the last word. I prayed aloud to God, shouting above the music, shouting above the laughter. *"Save me, Lord, from evildoers. They are always plotting evil, always stirring up quarrels. Their tongues are like deadly snakes; their words are like a cobra's poison. Lord..."*

"AMEN!" Dudley said.

My father dragged me into the garden and shook me until my head hurt. Then he left me under a sky bright with stars, so angry that I did not see her standing in the shadow of the house: the Lady Mary. I had not seen her for two years and then I had mocked her faith.

"You are direct in your speech, *pequenita*, and I like that." I turned round to face her and sank into a deep curtsy. Her likeness to my mother – her cousin – startled me, but although they were the same age, she looked older. There was no trace of Tudor colouring in Mary, thanks to her Spanish mother, Catherine of Aragon. Catherine lived on in her daughter's dark eyes and hair, and in her Spanish accent. "So you see my little brother still allows me to visit him, as long as I hide my faith inside my robes." She parted her jewelled black fur and fumbled inside her gold-edged collar, lifting up a rope of rubies which held a golden cross encrusted with more rubies, so red that blood seemed to seep from Christ's body. Then a rosary. I stepped back. Everything about her repelled me.

"I should prefer to stay in Hertfordshire where I am

allowed to pray to my God as I wish. At least the King understands that." Her hands fingered the ivory beads of her rosary as she spoke. "But, as you see, the King is not well and I must see him." She came towards me. "So you are not yet betrothed to my little brother?"

I shook my head. "I do not wish to be Queen of England, ma'am, although if the King wishes it, there is little I can do. I still fear that he will."

"You *fear* it! And that is all I wish, to be Queen of England and to bring this unhappy country back to the true faith. So fear is the cause of your unhappy face. I recognize it well, *pequenita*."

Her dark eyes looked me up and down. "Pearls are only as good as the skin that reflects them, Jane, and your skin is too pale." She took off the ruby necklace, unhooked her crucifix, and placed the rubies around my neck. "It will bring a bloom to your cheeks. It is yours as a keepsake."

I thanked her and she smiled at last. Then she closed her eyes and moved her lips, in what I assumed was silent prayer.

*　*　*

I longed to see Ned. I had missed him. Yes, I would go straight to the forest when we returned home. I had never been there at twilight. The trees would gleam red in the sunset, patterned by flocking birds.

I would meet him on his way from work, his axe swinging over his shoulder. My lips parted in a smile as I imagined his pleasure when he saw me, when I told him that I loved him.

Ned

She will be home tonight.

I smile to myself as I walk with Thomas. He strides among the trees, peering and prodding, until he comes to an elm edging the pool, so tall that I cannot see its crown. "This'll give us enough wood till winter," he says.

He scrambles up the trunk and onto the lowest

branch. There he raises his axe and chops. The branch falls easily. Thomas swings round to the other side of the trunk and raises his axe again. I hear the familiar creak, the rustle. Then a crack as the branch gives way too soon, throwing Thomas to the ground.

I drag the branch from him and wait for him to jump to his feet. He has often fallen further and lived to tell the tale, so he has always boasted. But he does not move. I kneel down beside him. No scratch. No graze. No blood.

Then I take the flask of water from my bag and lift his head. I know then that his neck is broken, snapped in a second, snuffing him out like a candle.

The birds continue to sing, the wind continues to stir the leaves. I glance around me and dig deep into my bag to find my rosary and crucifix. Then I place the rosary into Thomas's hands, murmuring, "I resolve thee from thy sins."

Suddenly I feel a priest's power surge through me and I hold up my crucifix in the slanting light and pray out loud: "Hail Mary full of Grace, the Lord is with

Thee. Blessed art Thou amongst women and blessed is the fruit of thy womb Jesus. Holy Mary, Mother of God, pray for us sinners now and at the hour of our death. Amen."

From the corner of my eye, I see a movement in the trees. "Who is there?" I call out, hearing the panic in my voice.

There is no reply.

Jane

A flash of silver in the dying light. I recognized Ned's hair at once as he knelt over a body on the ground. I moved forward, anxious to help. My eyes followed him as he sank back on his heels, pulled something from his bag and raised himself again onto his knees.

What was he doing?

Birds sang their evening song above my head as

shafts of moonlight glinted on the crucifix in his hand. His words pierced my skin like arrows, each one sinking deeper than the one before...*Holy Mary... Mother...sinners...death...* Words of the old faith.

Anger replaced the pain and it raged through my body.

Why had he not told me?

Like a hunting hound mad with the scent of blood, I burst from the trees and ran towards him.

Ned

Her eyes blaze as she looks down at me. "You should have told me!"

"Told you what?" I ask. "That we worship the same God? Does it matter how we do it?"

"*We* do not need all that clutter."

Her cruel words shock me. "Do not call it that! What has made you so intolerant? You have no doubt just seen your cousin Mary."

"And she repels me," Jane says, "with her garish gowns and glittering jewels." She sneers. "You would suit her very well. I do not need trinkets to speak to God."

I get up to touch the ruby necklace around her neck. "And what trinket is this?"

"The Lady Mary said it would warm my cheeks." She rips it from her neck and stuffs it in my pocket. "You should take it to her. *She* would make you very welcome."

She flinches as I raise my hand in front of her face. "Is *this* scar not proof enough of my faith? Is *it* not enough for the Lady Mary to see how much I have suffered in this ungodly land?" She steps back and I move closer so that she cannot refuse to look at my palm of puckered silver. "It was for one of those trinkets, as you call it, that I have already faced the fires of hell." I shiver in spite of my anger.

"You are not the only man to have felt the flames of hell," she replies calmly, as if I were a child. "The Lady Mary lives in Hertfordshire. You will see the house easily from the road. It is the only one in Hunsdon with a tower. Yes, go to *her*!"

Her cold confidence enrages me.

"Is that all you have to say?"

She half buries her head in her hands. "I came here to forgive you."

"Well, forgive me then! I accept your faith, Jane. So why can you not accept mine?" I reach out and touch her hair.

She does not stop me, but looks at me with softer eyes. "I do not know any other way, Ned. No painted saints, no incense, no candles. We Protestants have said no to all that. And the bread and wine of Holy Communion is just that. It does not change into Christ's body and blood."

"The Bible tells us what Jesus said the night before he was crucified: *'Take this bread in remembrance of me.'*"

She sighs with impatience. "And where was Jesus when he spoke those words? He was alive, at a table, holding the bread in his hands. That is all, Ned. Bread – not body!"

"What if you reformed thinkers are wrong? Have you *ever* thought of that?"

I shall never forget the look on her face. She gazes straight back at me, her head held proud, her hair streaming over her shoulders, a light in her eyes I have never seen before.

"A Protestant can never be wrong."

And she turns and walks away. I run after her, shouting. I do not care if anybody hears me. "Go on, tell them! Have me sent away. I do not care. Tell them!"

She turns for a moment, her face serene. "I shall pray for you, Ned."

"I can pray for myself." I glance back at Thomas, already pale in death. "He was a good man. So will he go to your heaven or mine?"

She does not answer. I watch her walk from the last sunlight into the trees and she is suddenly lost in the shadows, taken from me in that moment, turning my world cold.

Jane

"Perhaps it is for the best," Doctor Aylmer said.

I whirled round to face him. "For the *best*? How could it be for the best?"

"Do not tell me that you did not suspect. You are clever, Jane. You *must* have known. That is why you did not ask him."

I picked up my Bible. "I swear that I did not."

I looked closely at him. "*You* knew! You have both deceived me," I shouted. "He should have told me! *You* should have told me!"

At that moment, I became my mother. My lips thinned and turned down at the corners. I slapped Doctor Aylmer's cheek. He did not react, so I slapped him again, harder. Finger marks flushed his skin. Then I threw myself into his arms, sobbing. "I am sorry, I am sorry. That is what my parents have done to me. Violence breeds violence."

"You are upset, that is all." He sat me down because I was trembling. "Be calm, Jane. It was not for me to tell you. It was between you and Ned."

"How can there be anything between us now? He is a Catholic and I am a Protestant."

"Does it matter?"

I blushed and shook my head, ashamed.

"I have told you many times, Jane. You must not judge people by the way they pray to God."

"I liked being with him." I smiled to myself as I remembered. "And now I cannot be."

"Ask God to forgive you," Doctor Aylmer said. I knew that he was disappointed with me and that hurt almost as much. As he turned to go, he stopped and said, "It is never too late."

It was cold in the chapel. They had taken Thomas's body there and all evening a procession of people had come to pay their respects – everybody except Ned. Two small candles lit the coffin, now closed and covered with aconites, primroses and snowdrops.

I knelt to pray. What if we reformed thinkers *are* wrong? What if the bread and wine are the flesh and blood of Christ?

The door creaked and the candles flickered, but I did not turn round, even when footsteps approached the coffin, until the hairs on my neck prickled and I knew that Ned was there. He was placing ivy on the coffin, ivy for eternal life.

"Forgive me, Jane!" he said.

I turned to look at him. "The Bible says that the truth sets us free," I said, "but it is wrong. The truth teases and betrays." Revulsion filled me. "The lips that have touched mine are stained, tainted with Jesus' blood. Go away, and never speak to me again."

But he came closer. "It is still not too late, Jane. Remember what I said that day in —"

"You fool!" I shouted. "It is even more impossible than it was then."

"Why?" he said. "I will give up the priesthood for you. What will you give up to be with me?" He paused. "You could start by giving up your intolerance."

"I cannot help it, Ned. I *have* tried."

"Then try harder." He took hold of my hand, turned over the palm and kissed it. "Do you love me?"

I nodded. "But I do not love your faith."

"You do not need to. Come with me, Jane. Do not forget the life you want...the freedom...we can go..."

My father pounced like a wild animal. How long had he been listening? He came so close that I could smell the ale on his breath, see the morsels of meat between his teeth. He squeezed the skin of my arm between his finger and thumb, faintly, then harder so that my skin stained red. "Go back to the house, Jane," he said, his face mottled with anger. "Tell Mistress Ellen not to let you leave your bedchamber."

They came for him after dusk.

"Come out, Papist plotter!"

"No need to kill 'im!"

"Blood drinker!"

Flaming torches flickered as far as the bakehouse. There were about seven men waiting outside – one of them was Jack – all restraining the hounds.

"Out! Out! Papist spy!"

As Ned ran down the steps, the dogs hurled themselves at him, but he kept running.

I saw it all from my window: the snaking trail of flame skirting the forest, gusting in the wind, disappearing and reappearing, and all this time I thought of the dogs sinking their claws and teeth into Ned's fair flesh.

"Come away from the window." Ellie pulled me back, closed the curtains and rocked me in her arms.

"Let him go!" I said. "That is the price he must pay for all his deceit."

No, my head did not want him.

But my heart did.

My anchor had gone. Without it, I was tossed on wintry seas. I was alone. And sick at heart and full of shame.

I did not know who had seen us in the chapel. It could have been Jack or Alice, Catherine or Mary – or just my father coming to pay his respects one more time to his trusted servant. He would not tell me. He only taunted me for bringing a Papist to Bradgate Hall.

"Jack was strutting around the kitchen like a bird with a worm," Ellie said. "*He* would have known that Ned had gone to the chapel. Or Alice could have told him."

Alice flickered into my mind. I had watched her only yesterday, stumbling across the kitchen yard on swollen feet, her face lumpy and rounded. She had curtsied clumsily.

Has he trapped you, Alice, as he has trapped Ned?

But knowing who it was made no difference.

Ned had gone.

I felt a wound in my side that I knew would slowly heal with time, but like all wounds it would leave a scar as a reminder.

Although in my head I knew that Ned had gone, in my heart I did not believe it. I still went to the forest, thinking that I would glimpse him. They say that after someone has died, you seek their face for a long time in the crowd and that was how it was with Ned.

That January was the coldest Ellie could ever remember. Its shadows chilled us to the bone. Dusk brought snowflakes swirling from the hill and they settled lightly.

Where was Ned? Was he lying under a whitened hedgerow, face and fingers frosted?

One evening, I crouched in front of the fire. I did not want to move for Ellie to prepare me for bed. "I feel like death, Ellie."

"You think too much and too deeply," she replied,

lifting up my hair to brush it. "Your head will be so full one day that it will fall off."

I put my hands to my neck, horrified. "Do not say that!" I cried. "Not even in jest."

It happened that night just as Ellie said it would. Not to my head but to that other part of my body that is hidden and mysterious. I woke up so early the next morning that I thought the huntsmen must be gathering below my window. I dragged myself to the window, my body heavy and scented with a sweet smell I did not recognize. There was nobody there, only the horizon streaked with red. When I went back to my bed, I saw that the bed linen was spotted with blood.

You will only marry when you can have a child.

Now Ellie brought me strips of linen to bind my body. "You cannot change the course of nature," she said.

I pleaded with her. "Do not tell anybody."

"Your mother asks me almost every day and I cannot lie."

"Not today," I begged, "or I shall…I shall kill myself. Do you promise?"

She nodded.

I could not stop myself from weeping and I was surprised that my tears were not full of blood. Then I leaned my face against the windowpane and my tears melted the frost away.

Now I would face my fate as Ned was facing his.

Ned

They are like the black dog of my nightmare, the dogs that chase me. Two of them reach me and pull me to the ground, tugging at my clothes, snarling and slavering. But I push them off and I get up as soon as the grip of their teeth slackens. I run like a madman through the night until I realize that they are not following. The first night, I squat in a ditch, ready to run. It takes all my courage to stay.

Every rustle, every shuffle makes me jump. I hear whisperings in the dark. I cannot catch their words and I know they are all in my imagination.

Dawn brings soft sunshine and silence and I stretch my limbs, pleased with myself for still being alive.

What shall I do? The necklace reminds me, its sharpness prodding my skin. *Take it to her. She will make you very welcome.* Why not? The Lady Mary is of my faith and she will give me news of Jane. Yes, I shall go to her.

I stumble away from Bradgate Hall towards the Great North Road. Fear goes with me. Although I may no longer be recognizable as the boy who escaped from Lincoln prison, who stole a loaf of bread and an apple and nearly hanged, I know that if anyone finds the necklace, they will hang me from the nearest tree. I unpick some of the stitching of my waistband and thread the rubies through, and as I walk they dig into my back, reminding me constantly of why I am making this journey. Then I quicken my pace.

❀   ❀   ❀

I want to die many times during the silent and solitary days that follow. In the evening, when the trees darken with flocking birds, I allow myself to think about Jane. Only then. I have to ration the thought like my food, otherwise I cannot bear it.

I cannot remember the days now, only the weeks – and I pass them on the highway. I am not fit for this journey and the coins in my pocket remind me that I could hire a horse. But my fear of being recognized is still too great.

On the path to a village called Oakham, I catch up with a small boy as thin as a reed, his face smudged like a bruise. He does not leave me. He does not ask for food. He does not ask for water. He just wants to be with another human being. I soon get used to the pattering of his little bare feet. Sometimes I hand him a crust or a bad apple and he always takes it. Once the wind blows so hard that he falls over, he lets me carry him.

He has been alone so long that he has forgotten his name.

"I shall call you Tom after the great bell in Lincoln Cathedral," I told him and he smiled for the first time.

The next morning, Tom does not wake up. I wipe his face with icy water from the ditch and place him in the bulrushes, scattering him with violets.

I miss him, and his footsteps haunt me every mile. And I fear the cold. I know that a fit man can walk twenty miles a day in good weather. But the icy winds have weakened me.

The cold deepens every day, forcing me to light a fire. I flinch as the first flame flickers, and stand well back, piling on twigs with a long stick. The same stick secures a rat. Its roasting flesh sickens me to the stomach and forces the memories to tumble from me.

It was a day like this when they came to our house last year. My father was sitting at the fireplace. Blazing oak logs scented the air and wood ash speckled his hair as he leaned towards the flames, spilling water from his goblet, making them hiss.

There were three of them. As soon as they forced their way into the room, they went straight to him and ripped off the crucifix he always wore, so hard that I thought they had broken his neck. They hurled it into the fire and turned towards me, jeering, "A young Catholic in the making! Do you go to Mass with him?"

I did not reply.

"It is me you should talk to," my father said. "Leave the boy alone."

One of the men – I remember he had red hair – sniggered. "Boys are always a soft touch," he said.

I flinched at the menace in his voice. I had heard plenty of tales about what soldiers did to soften up Catholic boys and girls. The clock ticked. To my relief, they went back to my father. "Who goes to Mass with you?"

He just bowed his head. I thought they would arrest us there and then, but they seemed to lose interest. They glanced at each other, shrugged their shoulders and made for the door. I ran towards the fire, picked up the poker and started to push out the crucifix. The red-haired man happened to glance back. He whispered something to the others.

They all came back, forcing me to kneel in front of the fire, tugging my right arm until I thought it would leave its socket. Then they thrust my hand into the flames.

My father howled like an animal, but the pain was so great that I could not cry out.

"Take your precious crucifix!" they shouted.

I grasped the hot metal. I saw my hand blacken, smelled the stench of sizzling skin. The men laughed as they left. And I dropped the crucifix and slipped away into total darkness.

My father continued to wear his crucifix, proud of its twisted metal, proud of my bravery. But I was not brave that day. I had no choice.

Now panic fills me as I look at the fire I have lit. I glance down at my scarred palm and weep like the child I was that day.

❋　　❋　　❋

Spring is late and the trees start to green long after the end of Lent. The cold winds and rain make my bones ache and I long for the warmth of the bakehouse. A late frost nips the budding leaves around me and the daffodils bow their heads over the whitened grass.

I stagger along. It rains every day, a soaking rain, and a fever quickly grips me. The highway rises up to meet me and as I put out my hands to protect my head, I topple onto the side of the road.

I know that I am ill and I know that I am safe. Although the hands that help me are rough-skinned, they are also gentle and lavender-scented; except when I have to relieve myself and the woman with me shouts, "Walter, you're needed up here!"

One day, when the sun brightens at the window and strength seeps back into my limbs, the man helps me downstairs.

"It's summer," the woman says in a cheerful voice. "You've been with us more than six weeks. Is anybody expecting you?" I shake my head.

I judge the Palmers both to be nearing fifty. Walter Palmer is slight and anxious and it is his wife, Anne, who rules the roost. Her head is always full of plans and preparations. She consults the latest copy of *The Book of Husbandry* every day for helpful farming tips.

They have had a farm all their lives, but find it more and more difficult to get help with the work. "Young men these days prefer to beg or steal instead of earning an honest living," Walter grumbles good-naturedly.

"We had two little ones of our own, dead many years," Anne Palmer says, her voice wistful. "The lambs became our children."

"That daft young King has a lot to answer for," Walter goes on. "Never known so many laws. I can't keep up with them. Why don't he just leave it to us to decide?"

Anne pats her husband's arm as if he is a naughty child. "What he means, Ned, is that only this March the government says there are too many sheep in England and not enough land for growing crops. So now we've got to get rid of some of them and plough up the land again. Who's going to compensate us for all that work?"

"Why don't you stay the summer with us, Ned?" Walter asks. "We could pay you six pence a day and your bed and board – and plenty of noon meat." He glances at Anne and her cheeks flush. "We ask only one thing and you must answer with the truth." I stiffen and twist my fingers together. "We are of the new faith, Ned. Are you?"

How I want to nod my head and embrace them both as my new family! But I shake my head slowly.

Mistress Palmer goes into the house and comes back carrying a small parcel of cloth which she hands to me. Inside nestle my rosary and crucifix. I look from one to the other, puzzled. "But if you already knew, why did you…?"

"We wanted to make sure you were honest," she replies. "Better an honest Catholic than a dishonest Protestant. Will you stay and work with us, Ned?"

"No. I am sorry. I cannot. But God bless you for all that you have done for me."

It is time to leave, to go to the Lady Mary. Walter takes me to the Great North Road in his cart. With a sad wave he leaves me. Alone again, and with the sun on my right, I head south once more.

Jane

The forest burst into life at last. Cow parsley hid the stream once more and catkins unfurled as long as a spaniel's ear. Doctor Aylmer was sitting in the walled garden, watching Catherine and Mary as they threw pebbles into the fountain. I could see him from my window. I could see my reflection, too, and I was shocked at the pinched paleness of my face.

I ran down to him. He would understand my anguish. But I saw tears on his cheeks and my heart thudded. "What is wrong?" I asked gently. "You are very pale."

"A scholar's skin is always pale," he replied. His shoulders sagged as he turned and held my hand for a moment. "I am unhappy because *we* shall not be together much longer."

My mouth dried with fear. I had to forget Ned in that moment. "Why? Are you unwell?"

He shook his head, his eyes begging me not to ask any more.

"Tell me what is happening, Doctor Aylmer," I begged, gripping his hand so tightly that he winced. "I can bear it if I know. Knowledge is everything. You have taught me that."

"You will know, but not from me," he replied. "I, too, have to obey your parents, My Lady." He unfolded my fingers and held my hand to his lips and kissed it. Then he walked towards the house.

Mary ran towards me, laughing. She tugged at my

dress, almost pulling me to the ground. "I'm going to be married," she said. Her voice was high and excited.

I laughed. "You are only eight years old. You are too young."

"No she's not." Catherine's voice came from behind me. "We're *all* to be married."

Everything stilled around me – the birds, the insects, the clouds. I no longer smelled the flowers. Why had nobody told *me*?

"Marriage is as catching as the plague," I said. I scowled at Catherine. "So whom shall I marry, Mistress Know-All?"

Mary opened her mouth to speak, but Catherine shook her head. "I'm not telling," she said. "But it starts with 'g' and ends with 'd'." She laughed. "And it's not God." She pulled Mary from me and ran back to the fountain.

"Guildford!" I whispered to myself. I shuddered at the thought of his fleshy face. "But why should I marry Guildford Dudley and not the King?"

I did something I had never done before. I went into

my father's private chamber without being summoned – and I entered without knocking at his door. I did not know what I was going to say. Anger had stopped me from thinking. My mother was with him.

"I hear that I am to marry," I gasped out the words. "Is it true?"

"Yes," my father replied. "You are betrothed to Guildford Dudley."

I remembered my mother's words: *there are worse punishments than the whip.*

"I shall not marry him," I shouted. "He is a Dudley and all the Dudleys are devils, and like the devil he is a roaring lion come to devour me. His father cannot want this marriage. He cannot stand the sight of me."

"It is a good match," my mother said, coming closer.

"For whom?" I shouted. "For you? For his father, a man who rules the King with a rod of iron? I shall *never* marry him! He—" She slapped my face. "I shall not. I fear the father rather than the son."

My father got up and took down his whip from the wall. "Ungrateful daughter!" Spittle frothed at his lips.

"I am sick of the sight of your sullen face. You have royal blood running in your veins. It is your *duty* to marry." He raised the whip. "King Edward has agreed to this marriage. Do you dare to disobey him as well as me?"

My mother took the whip from his hands. For a moment her eyes seemed to soften and glisten. I almost forgave her then. But she whipped me as my father held me. She lashed only my back. "She cannot have bruises on her arms for her wedding day, Henry," she explained.

The whip cut through my flimsy dress and then I was more concerned that they should see my flesh than about the pain.

Please God, let me die. I do not want to live like this.

Ellie bathed my back with lavender water and the tears that fell from her eyes.

The marriage ceremony was to take place in London at my father-in-law's home – Durham House – which stood on the banks of the River Thames close to my parents' house.

I said goodbye to the forest with a heavy heart. The wind was strong in the trees, rattling the leaves. Clouds piled across the sun, dropping rain onto every leaf. My eyes searched everywhere for the darting black of the raven, but I did not see him.

We set off on a sultry May day, a long procession of horses and litters. The side flaps were open and I looked back as we curved around the forest. "I might never see it again," I muttered. I did not mean to say the words out loud. People do that on the scaffold before they are blindfolded. They say that you wear a blindfold so that the axeman cannot see his victim's eyes, but I think it is to deprive the victim of his last glimpse of the world that suddenly becomes very dear when you are about to leave it.

My mother glanced at Catherine, but neither of them spoke.

A raven came into sight, hovering above us. Suddenly, a black shadow blocked out the light. It was a hawk, skimming the sunrise. It turned and swooped. The raven could have escaped, I was sure of it. But he did not try. He glided gracefully through the air until the hawk caught him with his claws. Even then he did not struggle. I watched until they became silent specks against the sun.

Ned

The days are hot. I sleep in the shade by day and walk in the evening cool, and even during the night. Not many people are brave enough to travel by darkness, but it comforts me, like being back among the trees.

On the third day, a cool wind begins to blow from the east and I walk during daylight. Granite outcrops give way to hills sprinkled with trees. Hertfordshire is softer than Leicestershire. I have never seen a greener county.

Jane was right. I can see the towers of the house two miles from Hunsdon. It is an isolated palace for a princess, and difficult to believe that the Lady Mary, once the adored first child of the King of England, can live here.

A woman opens the door long after I have knocked. She speaks before I do and her accent is Spanish, and I remember that Mary's mother came from Spain. After her mother's death, and when Henry was married to Anne Boleyn, Mary became a prisoner. Yet she was allowed to keep a few Spanish ladies-in-waiting. A kind gesture for a terrified young girl. The woman's voice cuts through my thoughts. "Be off, unless you want me to set the dogs on you!"

"I must see the Lady Mary."

"She's not here."

"I am of your faith," I whisper. "Where is she? Please tell me!"

She glances around her, nervous, and begins to close

the door. "She set off for London yesterday because the King is ill. Then she changed her mind on the way and headed for Norfolk instead. Nobody knows why."

"Norfolk!"

"*Si, senor*. To Kenninghall. It lies east of Thetford forest, about two days' ride."

The need to see the Lady Mary has taken hold of me as quickly as the fever. I *must* have news of Jane. I am far enough from Leicestershire to risk hiring a horse. One shilling gives me a black mare which does my bidding all the way.

I have imagined this ride many times, riding through the fens towards the east coast and taking a ship across the North Sea – with Jane riding beside me as I saw her that first day.

Rain is already spitting from the Norfolk sky as I come close to Kenninghall – a pretty brick house with a moat and a drawbridge. Lightning gleams and the wind hurls down red hailstones, stinging my skin.

I have never seen a storm like it.

Two guards take hold of me immediately and push me through the Great Hall into a small parlour where a fire burns in spite of the stifling heat. A woman staring into the flames turns round at the sound of our footsteps. The guards bow.

"We found him lurking outside, My Lady," one of them says.

I am in the presence of the Lady Mary at last. The woman my father worshipped as much as the Virgin Mary. The Saviour of England's faith. Now she stands in front of me like a statue, stern-faced, dressed in blue, laden with jewels. Her ladies-in-waiting wipe her forehead with lavender water, rub her hands.

"Who are you?" she asks. "Have you come to tell me that Dudley's men are at the gates waiting to arrest me?"

My heartbeat quickens. "No, My Lady. My name is Ned Kyme and I am of your faith." I pull the necklace from my breeches and everybody in the room gasps. "This is the proof that I have come from the Lady Jane in friendship." The heat from the fire is suffocating.

She holds the rubies to her neck where they glisten like blood.

"But how can my necklace prove that you are of my faith? You have been sent by the most Protestant person in England, apart from my sister Elizabeth. How do I know that you speak the truth, Ned?"

Wind gusts down the chimney, spitting sparks from the fire. I stare at the flames, hypnotized, and hold out my hand to them. My fingertips feel their heat. I clench my teeth and force my hand further, feel the skin scorch.

The Lady Mary gives a cry of anguish and pulls me back. "I believe you, *pequenito*," she says, tears wetting her cheeks. "I am sorry, but I can trust nobody in this treacherous world, not even my own cousin now that she has allied herself with the Dudleys! The King stands no chance against them. They are like vultures waiting to devour him."

Even in her anger, she catches sight of the blank look on my face. "Dudley has scooped up Jane for his daughter-in-law. He has married her to Guildford.

He was sent sniffing around her at Christmastide."

NO! I cry inside my head.

The Lady Mary smacks her lips with pleasure. "Guildford Dudley is a simpleton. How my learned little cousin will hate him! He likes to hunt and play cards. He has never held a book in his hands."

It has happened! And I am only able to bear it because her worst fear has not come true. She has not married the King.

The Lady Mary mistakes my sad face for fatigue. A servant shows me to a bedchamber flooded with sunlight and I lie there until summer thunder rolls across the horizon.

I rouse myself when I hear the bell for Mass and the ecstasy of it eases my agony. Although King Edward allows Mary to say the Catholic Mass, it is only on condition that she goes to chapel alone. But now she ignores this. I fall to my knees and pray as I have never prayed before. I breathe in the incense as deeply as I drink ale and it goes straight to my head. But at each moment of the Mass, when the bread is raised, when the wine is raised, I see Jane's face – slender with flashing eyes – and her glorious hair.

Then I know that although I can live without an outward show of my faith, I cannot live without her.

Jane Dudley.

I tried out the name, trembling. I still could not believe it would happen to me. I glanced at myself in the looking glass before we left for Durham House. My bridal gown was clever. Its golden embroidery made me look tall and graceful. Pearls glinted in my hair, but my face was dazed and dull.

Our wedding barge was the most beautiful thing on the river that day. Early roses strewed its golden canopy and ivy curled around the poles that supported it. I trailed my fingers in the water and thought of Ned and his duckweed spattered chest, thought of the dangling catkin part of him and shivered. I hoped that Ellie was right. She said that Guildford and I would not live together as man and wife, not until my father-in-law decided.

I did not look at Guildford when the marriage ceremony began. Then thin shafts of light shone down on us like the bars of a cage and they grew thicker, suffocating and sinister. I felt their pressure against my spine and my head and I wanted to push them back. When the sun went in, they disappeared.

For the first time, I realized that Guildford was caught in a trap as much as I was. What dreams did *he* have? I turned to look at him. His profile was strong because his nose was high-bridged. I smiled. He turned and caught my smile, surprised and smiled back, a smile that softened his sulky lips. I could not love him, but I could pity him.

I hardly noticed the feasting and music and fireworks. I only relaxed when it was over, when my parents took me home. Ellie was right.

But fear wore me down. When would I have to lie with Guildford? When that happened, I would truly be his wife and there would be no going back. The hollows of my cheeks deepened and I saw the bones on my wrist sharpen and at night I bit constantly into my flesh. I became the thin and worried girl that Ned had first known. I liked it that way – no reminder of my recent happiness.

Ellie was instructed to keep me healthy, if not happy. She gave me strengthening herbs by day and passionflower to send me to sleep at night.

The June days were sultry and thunder threatened every evening. Then it began to rain. The Thames washed over our water steps, foaming like spittle, and at night, the wind shrieked around the house trying to force its way through closed windows. I put my hands over my ears to shut out its howling.

On the sixth day of July, the sky darkened early and

the wind suddenly stopped. Lightning streaked the river horizon lighting up the red hailstones that clattered against my window.

It seemed like the end of the world – and it was the end of my life as a child. Towards ten o'clock, I heard voices downstairs and I peered into the hallway.

Guildford stood behind his mother.

"Pasty little thing," she was saying. "She will never bear sons as I have, Guildford. That is what comes of marrying somebody who prefers God to people. All that learning has been bad for her. Fresh air, good hunting and red meat – that is what she needs."

Her words did not upset me. Such words hurt only when they are spoken by those we respect and I did not respect my mother-in-law. But they disturbed me for a few seconds, in the way an insect does when it settles on your skin.

I returned to my bedchamber, my mouth dry with anxiety. Ellie tried to rock me, her forehead crinkled with worry, but I stopped her. "You need not treat me like a child, Ellie," I said. "I know why they are here.

I shall do my duty as Guildford will have to do his. I fear the blood rather than his body."

Hair brushed and threaded with pearls. Robed in a silken gown. Skin scented with rose-water.

I was alone with Guildford.

His hands were trembling as he stood like a helpless child and I wondered if – at the age of almost seventeen – he had ever undressed himself.

"We have no choice, Guildford," I said. "It is better to do our duty and then it is finished. There will be no need for you to come to my bed again."

Yes, he is caught in this trap just like me, I thought.

But his reply crushed my compassion. "Where is your little Catholic boy now?" he asked.

Guildford and I became husband and wife in a few fumbling moments during which neither of us spoke. There was nothing to say. As he lay with me, I imagined that I lay with Ned and I bit deep into my arm, and that was the only blood I saw.

The sun shone the next morning, although the stench

of damp river mud sickened me. There was talk of little else except the Great Storm. The flood had drowned people sleeping by the river. Lightning had struck the steeple of the first church in London to hold a Protestant service. And a baby had been born with two heads. One Protestant, one Catholic, people said. But in truth they were just two babies joined at the waist, for they also had four feet between them.

I curled up on the window seat overlooking the river. I had given little thought to the night before. For me it had been another tiresome duty like curtsying and kneeling.

Sun streaked the sky, lighting up a barge at the water steps. When it was steady, a woman climbed out.

It was Mary Dudley, Guildford's sister.

She wore a short fur cape and jewels around her neck and wrists. Too splendid for so early, I thought.

What was *she* doing here?

I called out to Ellie, "Send her away."

"She will have come to find out if your marriage has been consummated."

"It is none of her business. Tell her that I am unwell."

As I spoke, I heard footsteps on the stairs and Mary Dudley walked straight into my bedchamber. I shrank back against the wall. "What do you want?" I asked. I did not curtsy.

She smiled at me, a forced smile that did not suit the severity of her face. "You are to come with me to Syon House, Jane."

Syon House was the Dudleys' country home, a few miles along the Thames.

"I cannot go," I replied. "I am unwell."

She smiled again, just long enough for us both to remember what had happened the night before. I flushed, angry. She put her hand on my arm. "You must come now. My father has sent me to bring you."

"Are you forcing me?" I pushed away her hand. "Have you brought guards with you? I shall tell *my* father."

"Your father and your mother are already there." She paused. "And so is Guildford, with my parents. There is nothing to fear, sister."

"That is what people say when they are hiding something," I replied. "I shall not come."

Mary towered above us both. "You have not understood me, Jane." She took hold of my face and turned it to her, hurting my skin. "My father has *ordered* you to come." She nodded at Ellie. "Bring the robe she wore on the evening of her wedding. Quickly!"

I always know when I am beaten, when it is time to give in. Just like the hunt, I allowed myself to be dressed. Mary Dudley did not leave my bedchamber as I stood to be robed. She supervised everything, glancing at my thin chest, at the faint scars on my arms.

Syon House is two hours' journey by barge. But the prettiness of the river journey could not console me that morning. There are some moments in your life you never forget as long as you live because they are so full of terror. This was one of them.

I sank back against the cushions and pretended to sleep. Mary Dudley let me, supposing, I imagine, that I was exhausted after my wifely duties. When Ellie touched my arm, I opened my eyes and saw the water steps of a large white house on the north bank. We climbed from the barge and made our way to the deserted entrance.

My father-in-law was waiting for us. He led me quickly to the Chamber of State, towards the throne on a dais where my parents were standing with Guildford. As we passed by, the men bowed and the women curtsied.

Dudley raised his hand for silence. "As President of the King's Council, I now do declare the death of his most blessed and gracious majesty, King Edward the Sixth, on the sixth day of this month."

My poor cousin! I was not surprised. I remembered his frail body, his gaunt face looking down from the gallery at Christmastide. Tears glazed my cheeks, but I held back my sobs. A thought came to me. The King had died on the day of the red hailstones. Why had we not been told then? And during the time that Guildford was in my bed, the King had lain cold in his.

Now I understood. I looked around the chamber for

the Lady Mary. My body relaxed a little. That was why I had to put on my finest robe: to meet my new Queen.

But I could not see her.

Suddenly, my father-in-law was standing right in front of me. His voice, as sharp as a whiplash, forced me to stare up at his cruel mouth. "Before his death, the King prayed to God to defend his kingdom from the rule of his bastard sisters, Mary and Elizabeth." He bowed so low that his head almost touched my hands. Then he stood straight, his face solemn. "The heir to the throne is by right your mother, the Duchess of Suffolk, the niece of Henry the Eighth. She has stood down in your favour. Before his death, King Edward named you, Lady Jane Dudley, heir to the crown of England." He turned towards the room. "Long live Queen Jane! *Vivat Regina!*"

My legs weakened. John Dudley had trapped me. I was his path to power. How skilfully he had hunted me – so skilfully that I had not even known. He had brought me to the place I had always feared most – the throne of England. I touched my neck, felt the blood beating wildly there. *How many blows of the axe would it take to kill me?*

"The crown should not belong to me!" I cried. "I do not want it. The Lady Mary is the rightful Queen."

A murmur of disapproval rippled through the room. I did not know what to do. In truth I wanted to hide behind the throne and put my hands over my eyes as I did when I was a child, thinking that nobody could see me.

"Do your duty, daughter!" my father shouted. Guildford stroked my arm. "I am here," he said. "Let me help you."

"I pitied you," I whispered, "but you have deceived me, too."

I turned to none of them – only to God in my fear. I knelt and prayed out aloud, "Dear God, please tell me what to do." There was no answer. "If you are there, God, help me. *Please.*" No answer.

So I sat on the throne of England.

Jana Regina.

Ned

A shrieking comes through the open windows of my bedchamber, so awful that it chills me to the bone. I am already awake. Horsemen have ridden in through the night and I lie wondering what news they have brought.

I run downstairs. The Lady Mary is sitting by the fire, her body racked by sobs. Suddenly she stops and laughs out loud. "All my life I have waited to bring this country back to the old faith!" she cries. Now her face is hard with hate. "*She* has taken it all from me. My own cousin." She turns and sees me standing there, open-mouthed. "I could have *you* killed now. Why should I not kill you? That is what I am asking myself, *pequenito*."

"What have I done, madam?"

"The most fervent Protestant in England sends you to me and *voilà*, now she is Queen, in my place. Do you understand, Ned? *In my place!*"

Sweat pours down my back. I want to be sick. "*Queen?* I do not understand! To be Queen, she would have had to marry your brother," I mutter, more to myself than to her. But the Lady Mary is used to catching whispers in the shadows.

"The King is dead!" she cries. "My poor little brother is dead!"

I bow in sympathy. "But how can Jane be the Queen? *You* have first claim to the throne."

"Dudley! The traitor Dudley!" she shouts. "He forced

Edward to agree before he died. A clever little plan. Now Dudley has all the power through Guildford."

My heart aches for Jane.

A pawn in a power game. How will she bear it?

In her anger, the Lady Mary amuses herself by attacking Jane. "I used to love her very much – the eldest daughter of my dear cousin Frances, the favoured wife-to-be of my dear brother the King. How could I not love her? I forgave her new faith as I had to forgive Edward and prayed to God to bring them back to the old ways." She leans towards me, her eyes distant. "She once mocked my faith, and in my own chapel."

"She was young and foolish then," I reply. "She would not say such a thing today. She would be ashamed..." I stopped, recognizing that the Lady Mary could be a powerful enemy. "It was wrong of her."

"In truth, I never loved her so much from that day, Ned. But she is family. And she has been tricked by her father-in-law." Her face grows serious. "There are going to be difficult and dangerous days ahead for her, and for me, *pequenito*. I am my brother's heir. But

Dudley does not want a Papist on the throne. My life is in danger." She seems to be speaking words she has rehearsed many times. "Dudley should have captured me before Edward died. That was his mistake."

She laughs suddenly. "The people *like* me, Ned. Many of them remember my father when he still loved my mother. The other wives counted for nothing."

Will Mary let me stay? After all, I have come from the enemy. And if she does not, where will I go?

Reassurance comes quickly. "It is not your fault, Ned," she says. "I know that. Stay with me and become a priest. The Catholic Church needs men like you. Yes, stay, *pequenito*! I like you."

I stay. But I am lonely. I am the only young man in her small entourage. Her ladies-in-waiting are jealous because she likes me, and angry that I do not flirt with them. Her advisors – only a handful – regard me with suspicion because I have recently come from the traitor Queen.

They think I am her spy.

They stop talking whenever I appear. But it suits me here. This is the nearest I can get to Jane and, if I am honest, a thrill runs through me when I remember that I am witnessing history in the making. When I am older, I can say to myself: I was there.

I do not know the Lady Mary well enough to guess what she will do. During the day, she broods in front of the fire; but in the evenings, she amuses herself by racing greyhounds sent by her supporters.

She loves them like the children she longed to have. I hate them – their thin backs bowed like old men, their ribs sharp under their skin. I back away, disliking their rough tongues on my hand.

But it is magical outside in the summer air. Flaming torches line the lawns leading to the orchard where canopies hang between the fruit trees. The dogs bark softly as I walk them out for a race. A young boy follows me carrying a bundle on his shoulder. "No hares are killed here," he tells me. "The dogs chase a hare skin stuffed with rags." Nor does the Lady Mary gamble for money, but for trinkets like handkerchiefs or ribbons or charms.

It cheers her. For the first time, I see her cheeks become soft and pink, her eyes shine with pleasure. I see the happy child she once was.

But my mind sees only one thing: Jane sitting on the throne of England.

Jane

I was so full of fear that I needed strong potions to stop me from shaking. Ellie bound my arms so that I could not bite them. So I bit the back of my hands. They bled, staining my wedding ring red, and my father-in-law ordered me to wear gloves. When I ran my fingers through my hair it came away in my hands and my skin tingled as if a hundred wasps had left their sting.

What had happened to the Lady Mary? There were rumours that she had smelled the snare and fled to Norfolk. Her face shadowed with sorrow haunted me.

"What will she have left, Ellie? I have taken away her hope and if you do that to a person you condemn them to unhappiness."

"You cannot change what has happened," she replied. "While you wait, it would be better to ask for God's help to accept the situation."

"Accept it?"

"What did the raven do when it was caught in the net? Did he struggle?"

"At first. Then he lay still. But he was waiting for death."

"No, he was waiting patiently so that he wouldn't damage his wings. You must do the same. You came along and freed him. God will do the same for you. The Lady Mary is no fool. She wants to be Queen as much as you do not want to be. Be calm as you wait."

"But if she has gone to the coast, what has happened to Ned?"

"You don't know that he's gone to her."

"Then where is he?"

She had no answer.

That night, as I slept, I soar through the sky as you do in dreams. Blood-red clouds tumble around me, releasing the sunlight over the white tower below me and I let myself drift towards it. A row of heads hangs over the Tower gate. Most are almost stripped of flesh, revealing yellowing bones. But one is new and the ravens settle on its tangled curls to begin their dirty work, perching on its forehead, leaning forward to pluck out Ned's eyes.

It is the custom in England for a new King or Queen to be shown to the people at the Tower by the River Thames. It is said to be one of the prettiest buildings in England, set between gabled houses and lawns sloping down to the water. Fields and forests enclose it. We arrived by barge in a small procession. I tottered through the gates. My mother had forced me to wear chopines tied to my shoes. I had let her because, for one moment, I had wondered what it would be like to stand three inches taller. But I could not walk in them without stumbling and, at a nod from my mother, Guildford steadied me. I hated his fat fingers on my arm, but he would not let go and I had to bear it.

It was not worth the trouble. There were few people waiting to greet us.

The royal apartments were in the White Tower and Catherine was there to welcome me. She sank before me in a deep curtsy.

"What was it like?" she asked, giggling. "You could be with child, Jane!"

My cheeks turned scarlet. "A marriage conceived by the devil and consummated by the devil's son fills me only with dread that I, too, may spawn a two-headed child."

She drew back from me in horror.

The evenings were the worst. Guildford and I ate under the royal canopy between my father and my father-in-law. Across the table sat our mothers. The relationship between two families is always difficult. After all, blood is thicker than water.

On the third evening, my father asked when the coronation would take place.

"When Guildford's crown is ready," my father-in-law replied.

I gasped. Only now did I fully understand Dudley's plot. I turned to Guildford. "You have no right to the crown and you will never have it."

"Guildford must be King," his mother insisted. "It is your duty to make him King."

"I have done more than my duty already," I said. "Guildford will *never* be King."

"I can see that my husband chose unwisely," she went on. "I warned him. Your parents should have beaten you harder."

My parents sat in silence and I hated them. I could not bear it any longer. I pushed my hands against the table, pulled myself to my greatest height and stared at the Dudleys until they all fell silent, one by one. My father-in-law was the last to stop speaking.

"Stop your squabbling!" I shouted. "I do not want to be Queen! You, Dudley, have deceived me as you deceived the poor King as he lay dying. You know that the Lady Mary is the rightful Queen. I shall hand the crown to her."

His face paled. "She is already in Norfolk, looking for a ship to take her to Spain."

"So you underestimated Mary's cunning!" I laughed. "The men of Norfolk never forgot your savage slaughter. She knew where their loyalty lay." I stared at them all. "The path we are treading is a dangerous one. We are walking through an unknown forest full of wild beasts who wait patiently for us in the dark. Did you not think of *me*? Go! All of you! Leave me alone."

They rose. My mother was the last to reach the door. "You have the makings of a fine Queen, Jane. That is what John Dudley saw in you."

Rage filled me. I heard Ellie take in a deep breath. I heard the rustle of her dress as she slowly rose to her feet. "How dare you!" I cried. "I do not want a man like that to admire me. He has made my worst fear come true. *He* has made me Queen of England. May God forgive you all!"

As my mother came back into the room, her arm raised to slap me, Ellie placed herself between us, quietly holding my mother's gaze until she left. Only then did I crumple and Ellie held me, her cheeks glazed with tears.

In the moonlight, I noticed for the first time a young oak tree planted on the green close to the White Tower. Its crown was thick with leaves and when the wind blew it leaned low, but it always sprang back straight and strong.

"Don't stand too firm, My Lady," Ellie said, "or *you* will topple over."

I walked alone every morning on this green. My weary brain played its tricks. I thought I saw Ned darting between the trees, laughing, beckoning, his hair silver in the rising sun.

One morning, I saw John Dudley in the distance coming towards me. Why was *he* here? I had to pass him because there was no other way to go.

He bowed. "Do you not have anything to say to the man who has made you the most powerful woman in England?" His clothes were different – more opulent, more regal. His short cloak was fastened with pearl buttons, his hat heavy with plumage. But I noticed as he straightened that a twitch on his left cheek betrayed his exhaustion.

I walked on. "Nothing that is fit for a Queen to say."

He laughed. "I like your spirit, Jane. I was not sure when I saw you again at Christmastide. You spoke too much to God for my liking. But you are strong-minded and that is the sort of woman my son needs. And so do the people of England."

"They want the Lady Mary."

"NO! They must not have a sickly queen who will persecute us of the new faith. She will destroy England." His eyes softened dreamily. "We can do great things for our country, Jane. Forget Guildford. He is a mother's boy. Work with *me*. Make England strong again."

"I did not know that it was weak," I replied. I began to walk away but he put out his hand to stop me. I paused. "Is it true that you plan to send men to capture the Lady Mary?"

He nodded.

I was alone for the first time with the man who had plotted and murdered, who was destroying my young life to satisfy his obsession for power, and who had taken me away from Ned. I raised my arm and pulled back my sleeve. As he watched, puzzled, I scraped the nails of my right hand across my skin. Blood bubbled from it. I wiped my hand in it. Then I smeared John Dudley's cheek. "You have used my royal blood!" I spat.

He glanced down at my stomach and then back to me and his lips parted in a taunting smile. "You could be with child." His eyes shone. "Imagine! A new dynasty of Dudleys! Then we shall have no need of you." I raised my hand to slap him, but he grasped my wrist.

I did not hear the raven until it was above us. It circled above Dudley's head, its wingbeat stirring the feathers in his cap. "Be off with you, devil bird!"

he cried. The raven swooped towards Dudley's hands and stabbed at them with its beak, over and over again, until he cried out in pain and let me go.

John Dudley, the Duke of Northumberland, the President of the Privy Council, my father-in-law: beaten by a bird.

Ned

She reminds me of Jane – determined and decisive. When word comes, two days after my arrival, that Dudley, four of his sons and three thousand men have already reached Cambridge, the Lady Mary prepares to leave for Framlingham Castle in Suffolk.

I do not realize the danger she faces until I see her dressed in black, hidden by a thick cloak although the sun blazes, crucifix and rosary and jewels all concealed. Her voice is strong as she calls me to her side. "Ned! Will you come with me on this dangerous journey...?"

Go with her, I tell myself, and you will know what is happening to Jane.

Mary is tapping her fingers on the table. "*Will* you...?"

I accept.

"That is wise of you, *pequenito*," she says. "Where else would you go?" She pauses, but I only bow and mutter my thanks. "Since I am old enough to be your mother that is what I shall be," she continues. "You will come with me as my son. If anybody asks, we are visiting your father's grave."

We are on the highway before the sun has barely cleared the treetops, riding like the devil, as if Dudley already pursues us, and we arrive as the last rays of the sun glint on the moat of the castle. Thirteen towers are silhouetted against the darkening blue and salt scents the air.

"You see, Ned, a perfect place for a siege!" she boasts. "My father gave me this castle. Perhaps he knew what might happen one day. And if Dudley comes too close, I can take a ship to safety – to Spain."

Men begin to arrive before dawn. I watch them all day. They come across the fields, a mass of men of every age. They each carry something they can use as a weapon; sticks, stones, knives, axes, scythes. The drizzling sky does not dampen their enthusiasm. They settle in the fields like locusts, eating and drinking and shouting, "I'm for Queen Mary!" By the third day, there are almost forty thousand men camped around us. Some move on towards Cambridge to meet Dudley, others stay to defend the Lady Mary.

She sobs and smiles and goes outside to pray with them, for them. She holds an open air Mass such has not been seen in England for more than twenty years, and not in my lifetime. I reel from the splendour of it all. Statues are hauled from the dungeons, dusted off and brought back to life.

As darkness falls, small fires light up the land. Then I pray for Jane constantly – pray to God to keep her safe.

Other men of noble rank ride up to the castle keep.

I hear them declare themselves: Sir John Mordant, Sir William Drury, Sir Thomas Wharton, Sir Henry Bedingfeld... Some have ridden from the west country, some from London, some only a few miles. Their names mean nothing to me, but I know now that they have all faced great danger to support the Lady Mary.

We are hearing morning Mass in the castle courtyard when the thought comes to me suddenly: if Dudley captures the Lady Mary, will he know who I am? If he finds out I have escaped from prison, I shall feel the rope around my neck for the second time. But it will not end there. I will be taken down, half-dead, and have my belly ripped open.

I am swaying on my knees in agitation, when horse hooves thud beyond the drawbridge. We all get up from our prayers to look. A single rider, clouded in dust, is forcing his way through the camp.

He declares himself: the Earl of Arundel come to tell us that Dudley has surrendered to Mary's men; come to tell us that he is loyal to her and nobody else.

The drawbridge is lowered and the Lady Mary goes onto the bridge to meet him. He dismounts and bows and his magnificent voice falters with emotion. "Dudley knelt down in the marketplace at Cambridge and swore his loyalty to you. The people want *you*. They never wanted Jane. You have been proclaimed Queen in London, Your Grace!"

Queen Mary raises her crucifix to the sky, her face streaming with tears. "At last, Lord!" she cries. "At last!" She takes a deep breath. "And the traitor Queen?" she asks.

Arundel's lips smack with satisfaction. "A prisoner, Your Grace."

My mind clouds over. Sweat gathers in the nape of my neck, dampening my shirt. My breath escapes in a long sigh. The Queen turns in an instant, her eyes flickering over me.

Then they leave me there. I stay on my knees and never have I prayed so loud and so long.

Jane

All day long – the ninth day of my reign – people pressed closer to the gates of the Tower and pelted the guards with sticks and stones. When the guards forced them back, they surged forward again. Now my fear of my people was as great as my fear of the Dudleys. I ordered all the gates and doors of the Tower to be locked and the keys brought to me.

"Save me, Lord, from evildoers. They are always plotting evil, always stirring up quarrels. Their tongues are like deadly snakes; their words are like a cobra's poison. They have laid their snares. And along the path they have set traps to catch me. Hear my cry for help, Lord!"

Why was my father not here to protect me? From time to time, I glimpsed him on horseback in the street. Then a cloud of dust rose up as he rode off again.

Everybody had deserted me, as Dudley's men were deserting him across England. The members of my Privy Council had left the Tower, each with his own excuse.

As the summer air grew chilly and drizzle clouded the sun, bonfires were lit outside. Church bells boomed across London and people sang as they celebrated in the streets.

That evening, I dined alone for the first time. Suddenly my father appeared in the doorway, tugging his beard, his eyes wild. I wondered if he had been drinking. He walked across to the table, reached above my head and tore down the royal canopy.

Jana Non Regina. Thanks be to God.

"So we are free of the Dudleys at last," I cried. My chest relaxed. I got up, dizzy with relief, and relief made me forgiving towards my father. "Can we go home now, Father? Please." He did not speak. Anger rose in me as it always did when he refused to answer my questions. "You are to blame, Father. What are you going to do to help *me*?"

He left without a word. I ran after him. "What about me, Father?" The guards would not let me pass. "What shall I do, Father?" I called again from the top of the steps. But he had gone.

Ellie came and I held her to me, crying and laughing at the same time. "It is over! It is over! I have been Queen for nine days and I have kept my head!"

"A puppy doesn't open its eyes for nine days," she replied. "But what will happen on the tenth day?"

I picked up my Bible and opened it at Psalm 124: "*'Let us thank the Lord,'*" I read out loud, "*'who has not let our enemies destroy us. We have escaped like a bird from a hunter's trap; the trap is broken, and we are free!'*"

A loud cheer sounded in the street. We looked through the window. My father was standing on Tower Hill calling to the crowd, calling out Mary's name and they cheered him. I waited for him to come back for me, but he climbed onto his horse and rode towards London.

I was still at the window when four guards came into the room. Their message was simple: I was now a prisoner of Queen Mary.

Ned

It is mid-afternoon when we reach London. The journey has exhausted us all, humans and horses. As we approach the city gates, a stench hits my nostrils, a stench of dirt and decay that rises from the River Thames curving to our left. I have never seen a river like this. It is so wide and so rough that foam floats on the water between the fishing boats.

At last I have reached the city where Jane is. I know that she is a prisoner and that I shall not see her, but I am happy just to be closer to her.

We have hurried for one reason: to see John Dudley brought to the Tower as a prisoner. The crowd presses forward, taking us with them.

I am now used to the sight of lords and dukes and earls – they have passed through my new life daily. But I have to confess that John Dudley is an imposing sight, even as a prisoner. A scarlet cloak covers him and, to my surprise, his sword still glitters at his thigh. Four of his sons ride behind him, cowering as dung spatters their father.

The woman in front of me has a pocket full of plums. She takes one out and throws it at Dudley's feathered cap. It wobbles, then falls off, and his rumpled hair shows grey. His horse slows down and for a second, I look into his eyes which seem to ask, "What am *I* doing here?"

No soft plums for me. I pick up a stone, raise my arm as if I am striking with my axe, and hurl it. My aim is true. He gasps as his skin splits open. His horse, feeling the reins slacken, bolts.

That is the last I see of him, lying low across his horse's neck, holding on for dear life.

It is that time of day when light is fading into dusk, when birds begin their nightsong, when the mind is prey to bitter thoughts.

Everybody has forgotten me! Where are Ulmis and Bullinger now? Ned was right. They were only interested in me as long as I was on the throne of England! Even my parents have not been to see me.

Be strong, I told myself. Queen Mary arrives in London tomorrow and she will surely set me free.

I glanced in the looking glass to remind myself who I was. I was startled. My brown eyes bulged in my thinned face, my hair hung limp and lustreless.

Would Ned still want me?

The streets, strewn with flowers, began to bustle long before dawn. Tapestries and banners fluttered from windows. People carried placards scrawled with Latin: *Vox populi, vox Dei.* "The voice of the people is the voice of God," I explained to Ellie. How different my arrival had been. These people wanted Mary as they had not wanted me.

As London sweltered under the hottest summer day that year and the Thames was shallow and stinking, trumpets sounded over the riverbanks and hoarse voices called out, "God save Her Grace!" A loud cheer rose up. Guards craned their necks. Ellie held me tightly as I leaned through the window.

Queen Mary's procession was magnificent. Hundreds

of men in velvet coats and rows of elegantly dressed ladies led the way, their dainty shoes crunching on the newly laid gravel.

Then I saw my Queen, her face shadowed by a jewel-trimmed hood, her purple velvet dress hung over a gold and pearl encrusted skirt. Behind her rode a beautiful young girl with long red-gold hair like mine, dressed from head to toe in white embroidered with silver leaves. Her green velvet headdress was studded with diamonds. The Lady Elizabeth.

As the Queen passed over the drawbridge of the Tower, I saw her face clearly. How thin it had become in the few months since I had seen her. Even her robes could not make her dazzle. Her face was marked with an unhappiness as deep as my own.

Then I saw Ned.

He was riding a grey horse behind the Lady Elizabeth. The last time I had seen him he had been a shadow in the chapel, whispering to me in the candlelight, filling my head with words I wanted to hear: love, freedom, a future.

He rode tall and straight, looking ahead as he had that first day. He did not turn his head to the crowd like Elizabeth, who always sought attention. Blue, green, silver. These colours flashed in front of my eyes, as bright as a peacock's.

My heartbeat quickened at the sight of him. Did he know where I was? Did he know that I was watching him as I used to from my bedchamber? I waited, holding my breath.

As he neared the White Tower and the procession slowed, he put his fingers to his lips.

How strange it was! The Catholic Queen living opposite the former Protestant Queen, unable to face each other, like the poor twins born on the day that Edward died.

I did not see Ned again.

And three days later, the royal party left for Whitehall Palace.

Why had she not released me?

❋   ❋   ❋

John Dudley climbed Tower Hill wearily, pausing at the scaffold to speak; but the people mocked him and screamed for his death. I had never felt such a tangle of emotion. It was wrong to kill, I still believed that. That is why I had saved Ned from the gallows without knowing what crime he might have committed. That was why I had derided Dudley at Christmastide.

I will not make an exception now, I told myself. I will not.

I knelt down to pray for Dudley's soul.

But as the roar of the crowd rolled around the hills like a summer storm, I got to my feet and rushed to the window. The axe glinted as it rose once, then twice, and the axeman held up the head.

Dudley's eyes would never dart up and down my body again. His nose would never sniff out power again. And his lips would never tell me again what to do.

My fingers gripped the edge of the windowsill. "He has caused great misery to me and my family through his ambition," I cried. "His life is odious to me. It was

full of hypocrisy and so was his death for he gave up
the new faith with his dying lips so that he might live
another day."

Ellie scolded me.

"Why should I not condemn my enemy?" I asked.

"Walls have ears," she whispered, "even if they are
covered in tapestries."

My relief did not last long. Dismal thoughts came to
plague me: Ned is with his Catholic Queen, drinking
blood and eating flesh, and it repels me. He will no
longer want me. His faith will plump out his feathers
and he will preen and strut as they do.

"Ned's a faithful person!" Ellie said.

"But you never liked him."

"Yes, I did, although I did not think your friendship
was wise because of your father. But look where that's
brought you! And has your mother pleaded for you as
she has pleaded for your father? No! I wash my hands
of them all."

"Why does Ned not come to me?"

"You're a prisoner, my little one. Ned can't ask for special favours. Have you forgotten what it is like out there? Tittle-tattle, plotting and power games, just as it was when Edward was King, and when you were Queen. Only the players have changed. Not the game."

Ned

I *must* see her.

When we arrived in London, I was foolish enough to think that the Queen would let me see Jane. I did not allow myself to think that she had a husband, also in the Tower.

Not only was I foolish, but I was naïve. I had forgotten that Mary was now the Queen of England.

And soon she was no longer a bastard child. I was too young to remember the time when Henry the Eighth had divorced Mary's mother to marry Anne Boleyn. But my father often spoke of Mary: how her parents' marriage had been annulled; how she had been declared a bastard. Immediately after her coronation, soon after our arrival in London, Queen Mary's first Parliament declared her parents' marriage legal again.

I am living at Whitehall Palace under the guidance of a man called John Feckenham. He is now the Dean of St. Paul's and he will decide whether I am suited to the priesthood. I like him. He has a sensitive face, and his skin is grey around his neatly clipped beard – the skin of a man who has been shut away from the sun.

The day we came by barge to Whitehall, the beauty of the palace took my breath away.

"Whitehall Palace is not just a royal home, Ned," Doctor Feckenham explained. "It is also the seat of government. It is like a small town. Anybody can walk in the public rooms and the gardens if they are well dressed and well behaved. But you must remember one thing: the Queen has to protect her privacy. The Lord Chamberlain has drawn up a strict list of rules. Anybody found in the wrong part of the palace will be punished."

Was he warning me? Was he reminding me not to ask for any favours?

"Where does the Queen live?"

"In rooms called 'the secret places'. I can go there. You cannot."

The luxury of my life from that day on astounds me. Sometimes, as I lie on my bed gazing at the painted ceiling, the thought comes to me, *Why did King Edward need to ruin my home when he had all this?* Then I close my eyes and see my childhood bedchamber once more: the carved mantelpiece, the statue of the Virgin Mary to the right of it. I can smell the candle that always burned there.

I am protected from the dirt and din of the London streets, although the smell of the Thames is always there to remind me that every stream that flows through the city brings its own share of filth. I rarely leave the palace, except to go to Mass at St. Paul's Cathedral.

Faith consoles me. As John Feckenham takes me under his wing, my passion for the priesthood returns and he sees it. I pour out my story to him. "I was born in a forest," he says with a smile. "Feckenham Forest, in the county of Worcestershire. I am the last Catholic priest to be named after the place they were born."

I lose myself in the rapture of the Catholic Mass again and again. The pleasure of seeing the bread raised at the altar as Christ's flesh is like water to a thirsty man wandering in the desert; the pleasure of my first confession for many years like being reborn.

But underneath, there is a restlessness which I cannot contain.

I *must* see her.

Autumn fills me with gloom. It has blown in on a gale, stripping all the leaves. It is unbearable in London. No wood smoke scents the air, only the foul stench of coal watering my eyes, prickling my nose.

We are walking in the gardens, John and I, the ones

made of coloured gravel divided by green and white railings – the Tudor colours – and posts topped by heraldic beasts. Beyond, across the road called King Street, I can see men playing tennis.

Feckenham walks me quickly, until we are alone. Then, for the first time, he asks me about Jane. Sometimes, as I talk, he places his hand on my arm and says, "It is not so terrible in the Tower. I hear that her gaoler is called Master Partridge and he and his wife care for her well."

I smile at the name. "It is the thought of her fear that I cannot bear," I reply. "She does not know whether she will live or die. And she is afraid of a botched death. I wish I could see her."

"Do you love her more than God, Ned? Or do I have a future priest in front of me?"

"I do not know," I whisper. "It is more than six months since I saw her. Only two miles separate us, but we are in different worlds. And she is married – I keep forgetting."

He glances around and lowers his voice. "The

Queen allows me to visit her. She hopes that Jane will turn back to the old faith."

"You are wasting your time, John."

"Perhaps, but we have become good friends. She is lonely and has enjoyed our discussions…"

"…which are all about the bread and the wine!" I cut in.

He nods. "Would you like to see her, Ned?"

Happiness rises inside me, but I am suspicious. "Why would you risk such a thing for me? You are supposed to be persuading me to the priesthood!"

"You have to be sure of your feelings." He hesitates. "Be up early before dawn, Ned, and wait for me at the water steps. Cover yourself."

I lie awake all that night. I see Jane riding beside me, the wind showing the shape of her body; I see her glorious hair streaming behind her, her slender face alive with flashing eyes.

Barges are already jostling for space on the river as dawn is breaking. I do not notice the journey, only that my hands are trembling so violently that I have to hide them under my cloak. I peer into the water, shocked by the look in my eyes. It matches the look I used to see in Jane's.

We reach the Tower. Under its walls lies an archway dripping water – Traitors' Gate – where ravens blacken the sky above the rotting heads spiked there. The ravens always gather at the Gate to feast. They peck the soft parts first – the eyes and the lips. Then the nose. And soon the head is no longer human, just a grinning skull.

One day my life might hang by a thread. For the first time, I truly realize the danger that Jane is in.

She did not know that I was coming. She sits huddled by the window, dressed in dark grey, her shoulders slumped in a way I have never seen them. I notice that her thin cheek still bears the imprint of the leaded glass. Fine lines mark the corners of her eyes. She looks older, but not prettier. Her face is pinched by sadness.

Her book slides to the floor as she sees me. She waits for me to speak, but I cannot find the words. I just sit at her feet and our shadows flicker and we could have been talking in the forest twilight. It gives me the courage to speak. "I have missed you."

It is enough. She holds me. "Where have you been?" She does not wait for my answer. "They have all deserted me, Ned. My mother, my father, Catherine, Ulmis, Bullinger. It is a strange thing, but all the Protestants I have known lately have shown themselves to be cruel. That is the hardest thing of all." She stops suddenly, her eyes resting on my crucifix. "I am sorry. What my father did was wrong."

"It does not matter now."

"Your faith suits you, Ned. Look at me, all skin and bone and you...!" Her eyes fill with tears. "You will not want me now! I do not know what will happen to me, Ned. It is better that you forget me and become a priest."

I shake my head. "The Queen will not allow you to die, Jane. She is your cousin. And when you are free, we shall leave England."

"You need people of your own faith, Ned. I can feel your faith still burning like a fire inside you. Accept it as

I accept mine. Do not deny God. He will not deny you."

"I am used to lying low in the shadows. I can do it again."

She leans forward and kisses me, a kiss like leaves fluttering against my skin. I kiss her back. "None of it matters, Jane, except my love for you. Statues, incense, prayer books, Bibles…they are all made by man."

The silence that follows is broken only by the sound of Ellie weeping quietly.

Fear, deep and dark, engulfed me. Only Ellie's arms stopped me from fainting to the floor.

I am to stand trial for treason – with Guildford and his brothers. Not my father. He has already been pardoned and fined twenty thousand pounds.

Following tradition, Guildford and I walked from the Tower to the Guildhall, he a few steps in front of me and in front of him, four hundred guards carrying halberds, that most cruel of weapons: half sword, half axe. So many men, and just for us. Ellie was not allowed to go with me and it was like leaving my shadow behind.

I could not look ahead, for the Gentleman Warden of the Tower walked in front of us, his blade turned away from us in a symbolic gesture. And I could not look to the side, for people jeered and shook their fists and called out, "Traitors!" So I read from the Bible at my belt, but Guildford stumbled so often that he fell into line with me. He was almost crying.

"This is my father's fault," he said.

"And my father's too!" I replied. I pushed him away from me. "Do not shame me by crying in public."

We pleaded guilty. We had no choice. After all, I had worn the crown of England, although against my will.

Guildford gasped as the sentence was given. Hung, drawn and quartered.

I stood still. Burning or beheading, whichever the Queen decides.

As we walked back to the Tower, the executioner's blade is turned towards us. When will it be? Today? Tomorrow? Next year? It will hang over me until... I shiver. A wind was blowing across the river catching the last leaves and they lay on the ground like pools of shining blood.

Ned

This morning, the Queen summoned me to her Presence Chamber. It is many weeks since I have seen her and she has changed. I know already that she has decided to marry King Philip of Spain and unite two Catholic countries, but I do not know how much love has softened her.

She tells me that she has decided at last: she will free Jane.

"The trial was only for show," she explains. "I had to prove to the people that their new Queen was made of stern stuff. Now they have forgotten all about it."

I tremble. "And Guildford?"

"The marriage will be annulled." She smiles. "*You* should have told me how you felt about my little cousin, Ned, not Doctor Feckenham. I would have understood."

I kneel and kiss her hand and thank her all muddled up together.

"I think we have just lost a priest." She laughs kindly. "But I am so happy that I want everybody to be happy."

"May I tell her, Your Grace?"

She frowns and I take a deep breath as she replies, "*Si, pequenito. Si.*"

Snow softens the winter bleakness as I arrive at the Tower. Everything is white, glinting in the frost, mingling earth with sky, silencing all sound.

They have given us fifteen minutes together in the Queen's garden. As I wait for the guards to bring her, I watch a raven huddling on the oak, half-hidden by a creeping mist. Snowflakes swirl around his head, sticking to his feathers, softening the branches even more.

She is dressed in black, pearls at her neck, a hooded cloak. I swirl her round until my head is giddy. "You will have to wait for your paradise. Queen Mary has forgiven you!"

Her frown deepens. "For what, Ned? A life with Guildford! I would rather die!"

My heart turns over with love for her. "The Queen is annulling your marriage to Guildford. You will be free, Jane."

She stands still with shock. "So we shall both have what we want," she whispers. "I shall be free of the Dudleys. You can be free in a Catholic England. Who would have thought it, Ned? God has finally answered our prayers."

A hissing like the sound of angry geese forces us to turn round and look up. High on the roof of the Beauchamp Tower stand the Dudley brothers, mingling with the ravens already perching there. Each wears the black of mourning like snow spattered feathers ruffled by the frosty wind.

We turn our backs to them.

The clock on the White Tower chimes once and the guards come to claim her. Jane clings to me. "When will they let me leave?"

"Shush…do not think about that now. Soon."

"Where will I go?"

"Across the sea! With me!"

"Imagine not seeing any land! What if I am seasick?" She holds me once more. "I am nearer to my dreams of freedom than I have ever been, Ned. They will not slip away from me this time."

I kiss her. "No, I shall not let them. You shall live the life you want. Until I see you again, may God go with you."

"And with you," she replies.

They take her in. I stand there until the next chime, until the snow hides her footprints as if she has never been there.

Jane

Whispers reached me through the January mists, through cracks in the walls, through gaps in the tapestries, forcing me to look across the river, hoping that the men I could see were the ghosts of my imagination and not Protestant plotters. There were many Protestants who did not want Mary on the throne of England. I had always feared they would rise against her and put me back on the throne.

Now I faced my fear. Thomas Wyatt's men, arrived from Kent to overthrow Mary, thronged the banks of the frozen Thames, unable to cross London Bridge because the Queen had ordered four houses in the centre to be destroyed.

Some of the men tottered onto the ice, confident until they were half-across and it creaked and cracked, plunging them to the river bed, already ice-blue. The men behind them scrambled back to the bank. Then, with great weariness, they trudged away, towards Richmond, to another bridge.

Worry furrowed Ellie's face like a winter field. She knew my misery and had matched it with her own as she heard me weep, heard me tear at my skin with my nails.

That evening, a single halo circled the moon. Always a sign of a storm, Ellie warned. The sky over the Tower deepened to orange and the ravens fell silent. All night long, hailstones drummed on the glass and the wind howled, and as soon as it was light, I ran to the oak tree. It was still standing proud and straight, but at its crown was a gaping hole. I fell to my knees on the muddy ground and wept.

The raven made his way carefully through the debris. I held out my hand, hardly breathing, and it came to me, its feathers lustrous in the rain, its beak open to drink in the droplets.

"Be off with you, devil bird!" The raven flew off and I looked up to see a tall man in the mist. I thought it was John Dudley's ghost and in a sense it was, because Guildford loomed in front of me.

"What do you want?" I asked.

I did not know that he was capable of such anger. The words spilled from his bloodless lips like berries from the raven's beak. "Innocent Lady Jane, misunderstood and badly treated, weeping in her tower for her loss of freedom, Lady Jane who never wanted to be Queen…" He stopped for breath. "Oh you are clever, My Lady, far cleverer than I am. You are on a par with my father. You are two of a kind. But you have put us both in danger now. I curse the Greys and the day I ever met them!" His anger astonished me. Then he cried, making no effort to wipe away his tears and they splattered to the ground.

"What have I done, Guildford? Tell me!" I moved closer and I smelt his fear.

"No! You tell me!" He spat in his rage.

"I do not know what has happened, Guildford, and that is the truth. If you know, tell me, I beg you."

My words calmed him. "Your father is being brought to the Tower as a prisoner." I steadied myself against the oak. "Whilst Wyatt was marching on our city gates, he was in Leicestershire – raising an army…to overthrow Queen Mary, along with Wyatt. He wanted to proclaim you Queen again." His lips curved into a sneer. "You may as well lie down over that oak branch now and let them chop off your head."

I did not remember how long I stayed there, only that Ellie came to me and draped a cloak around my shoulders. "My father has betrayed me a second time," I muttered. She rubbed my hands and feet, gave me hot milk and honey, pinched my cheeks to bring back the blood.

But I was lifeless.

I learned later that when he failed to raise an army, my father ran away and hid in a hollow tree where hunting dogs sniffed him out.

He had truly lost his head. And now I could lose mine. Terror consumed me.

"Soon my life will hang by a thread," I whispered to Ellie. "How many blows of the axe will it take to kill me?"

Ned

I cannot sleep for all the commotion. Cutting, sawing, hammering. There are gallows everywhere for Wyatt's men, stark against the winter sky – even in the churchyards.

London is loud with the dead and dying.

Hangings punctuate the day like the chimes of a clock. Some call to God, some cry for their mothers and some curse, but death comes to them anyway and their bodies stiffen, frosted within the hour like sweetmeats, their eyes glazed like berries.

Bodies sway in the breeze as far as I can see. A leg, an arm, a face, touching and turning in a deadly dance, their clothes fluttering like the last leaves.

I can never forget that I was almost one of them the year before last.

I have heard it all. Thomas Wyatt is in the Tower. Jane's father is in the Tower. Jane is… I cannot even think it.

The Queen is in the chapel and I wait until she turns to leave. Then I stretch out on the floor and clutch the hem of her dress. "Forgive her, Your Grace. Her father is a vain ambitious man. She did not know what he was doing." I look up at her. "And you, Your Grace. You are her cousin. Families do not desert each other in times of trouble."

She looks back at me with desperate eyes. "You are still such a child, Ned. Do you not know that the most dangerous enemy is your own family? They can hate you as suddenly as they can love you." She smiles, her eyes vacant as she looks down at me. "And the cruellest thing of all, Ned, is that Jane will not forsake her faith for love of life. You shall not see each other in the life after death."

I open my mouth to scream. But I have to stop myself. There is no going back now. I know that. I have to ask her one last favour.

She nods, eyes brimming with tears, and walks away.

Jane

The clock strikes midnight. The twelfth day of February in the year of our Lord, 1554. It has come at last. My death day.

Beauty comes to the Tower on moonlit nights such as this. The white-washed walls shine and the moat sparkles. The moon is full, lighting up the oak scaffold. They have killed a living oak for me and its pale wood will be stained with my blood. I shudder to think that it will be spilled for all the world to see. I shudder to think that they will hold up my head and call me a traitor.

I was right. Wife. Queen. It has brought me to my knees, though not in prayer.

A visitor came to me last night.

Dear Doctor Aylmer.

He knelt before me, kissing my hands, his cheeks glistening. When he rose to his feet, I saw that his eyes had dulled as if he no longer wanted to wonder at the world. I threw myself into his arms.

"How can the Queen do this to you, Jane? How can she kill *you*, her own cousin?"

"How can she *not* do it?" I reply. "She has to protect her kingdom from fools like my father – and me. Through no fault of my own, I am her greatest threat. She has no choice and I forgive her for it. In her eyes, I am a traitor. But what hurts me most is my mother. She begs daily for my father's life, but not for mine." My heart lurched. "You are not a prisoner here, too?"

"No! But I am too outspoken to live under a Catholic Queen. I am going to Zurich to join Ulmis and Bullinger."

"They forgot me," I said.

He embraced me tightly and spoke the words that Socrates uttered just before he took poison. *"I pray that the removal from this world will be a happy one. That is my prayer. So may it be."*

I touched his wet cheeks. *"I have heard that one should die in silence,"* I continued. *"Come now, calm yourself and have strength."*

I went to my little table, pulled open the drawer and took out sheets of writing paper. "I have written everything down. One day, I may be just a sentence in a history book. I want everybody to know the truth about what has happened to me."

He put out his hand to take them, but I shook my head. "Wait until my story ends. When it does, I shall entrust them to Mistress Ellen."

Doctor Aylmer pulled his hood across his face and left me as quietly as he had come.

There is much to be done, for dying is a busy occupation. I write to my father first. Although I am angry, I forgive him, for he has surely brought about his own death and we do not want to quarrel about it in heaven.

I delay writing to Catherine. I cannot bear to say goodbye to her. I leave her my prayer book and I write on the blank pages at the back: *I have sent you, dear sister, a book. It will teach you how to live and how to die. By losing my life, I shall find eternal happiness. We shall meet in heaven when it pleases God to call you.*

There are no words I can find for my mother.

And for dear Ned? A lock of hair.

My last dawn. On frosty mornings like this I used to walk in the forest to find Ned. My only regret is that I shall not die in its cool and green.

A sickly stench fills the air. Bodies have been cut down and boiled, leaving space for those about to die. London is laden with bodies.

The chapel bell tolls at mid-morning and grey clouds line the sky as Guildford goes to the block. I do not see him die but soon a cart rattles under my window and I glimpse his body wrapped in blood-soaked blue, his head placed next to him. Ravens crowd the edge of the cart.

Oh Guildford, the bitterness of death! Will they wipe the axe before they kill me or will our blood mingle in death?

The raven never leaves my window. "Do not attack the axeman," I tell him. "I want to die with dignity. Stay with me until they take me away for burial. Then you will be free to go."

Black velvet dress, black cap, black gloves. We are two black beauties, the raven and I. One who will live and one who will die.

Ellie bustles around the chamber folding and tidying, although there are other servants who can do this – until she is forced to stop because there is nothing left to do, until she is forced to face me.

"I am ready to die, Ellie, for it is clear I shall never

be free on earth. Soon my soul will be free of my troublesome body for ever. It will soar into the sky and enter God's kingdom gladly through gates decorated with pearls. I shall be free, Ellie!"

She gives a harsh cry like the raven when he was caught in the net. It echoes around the chamber and dies away. She does not make another sound, but her body stiffens as if part of it has already died.

"Remember that I go to another paradise, Ellie. It has been a long and dangerous journey to reach it. And we shall meet there, Ellie, for we have done nothing wrong in this life." I push her from me. "Will we still recognize each other? We do not know what death will do to us."

I take off my pearls and fasten them around Ellie's neck. "I shall know you by the pearls you wear." Then I take her into my arms and rock her and her body feels as frail as mine. "Goodbye, faithful friend. I shall weep no more for this wicked world, but I shall weep for you."

The chapel bell tolls again.

It is time. Men have manipulated me all my life, all except Ned. Now they come to murder me.

Will I see him in paradise? According to our faith – no!

Before I write my name for the last time, I ask only one thing.

Remember me.

Ned

Jane turns towards my hooded head and I almost stop breathing. I have imagined this moment many times since I decided.

I turn my hand from the axe, palm outstretched, its silver scar catching the light, and she understands. She smiles and her little white teeth shine like pearls and I notice that her neck is bare.

The people around us fall silent as she unties her glorious hair, lighting the winter grey like the day I had first seen her; and they lean forward to catch her whispered words, which they take to be her last prayer: "There is no place on earth for me, dear Ned. I shall only be truly free after my death. But do not wait for death to free you. Strive for freedom as long as you live."

A single blow. That is all I can do for her. Nobody else could have despatched her better to God. She was right. My freedom has come on earth, and I hope that hers will come in heaven.

Jane lies on the block until evening and I am amazed that so much blood can come from so small a body. But no raven pecks out her eyes or tears at the strips of flesh hanging at her neck.

As soon as they have taken away her body, I set out on the road north from London where I know the fine forests of England will shelter me – for now.

Author's Note

I have been interested in Lady Jane Grey ever since I was a girl – but she was always just a line in a history book: the unlucky Nine Day Queen. How did she feel when her parents beat her? What did she think when she was forced to become Queen through a loveless marriage? How would she have felt if she had met her soulmate and fallen in love? I wrote *Raven Queen* to try to get to know her better.

My research took me into a time of bewildering religious change: from a world dominated by Henry the Eighth, who steered England away from the Roman Catholic Church, to a Protestant England ruled by his son, Edward – and back once more to a Roman Catholic England when Edward's sister, Mary, became Queen after his death.

The Dudleys, Doctor Aylmer, John Ulmis and Mistress Ellen were real people. Ned is not.

Jane was a spirited and inspirational young girl whose life was sacrificed when she was only sixteen to satisfy a lust for power. If you visit Bradgate Park, where the ruins of her home still stand, you will see that flowers are always left at the gate on the anniversary of her death.

Raven Queen is for all those who seek personal freedom. Do not forget her.

Pauline Francis

Bibliograpy

Bindoff, S, *Tudor England*

Brears, Peter, *Food and Cooking in 16th Century Britain*, English Heritage, 1985

Davey, R, *Lady Jane Grey and Her Times*, British Library, 1911

Davey, R, *The Sisters of Lady Jane Grey*

Davies, CSL, *Peace, Print and Protestantism 1450–1558*, Paladin, 1977

Elton, GR, *England Under the Tudors*

Forsyth, Marie, *The History of Bradgate*, The Bradgate
Park Trust, 1974

Howard, G, *Life of Lady Jane Grey*, 1822

More, Thomas, *Utopia*, Everyman, 1974

Picard, Liza, *Elizabeth's London*, Phoenix, 2004

Plato, *Phaedo*, Oxford World's Classics, 1993

Plato, *The Republic*, Penguin, 1955

Plowden, Alison, *Lady Jane Grey: Nine Days Queen*,
Sutton, 2003

Ridley, Jasper, *The Tudor Age*, Robinson, 2002

Stevenson, Joan and Squires, Antony, *Bradgate Park:
Childhood Home of Lady Jane Grey*, Kairos Press, 1999

Taylor, A, *Lady Jane Grey and Her Times*, 1908

Weir, Alison, *Children of England: The Heirs of King Henry
VIII*, Pimlico, 1997

$\mathcal{P}auline\ \mathcal{F}rancis$ has worked as a school librarian and a French teacher, and spent time in Africa translating books before becoming a writer herself. She has written educational stories, such as *Sam Stars At Shakespeare's Globe*, focusing on her favourite subject, the sixteenth century, and retold classics such as *Oliver Twist*. She has also written for young people learning English as a foreign language. She returns to the sixteenth century in *Raven Queen*, her first novel.

Pauline is married with two grown-up children, and lives in Hertfordshire.

To find out more about Pauline Francis, visit her website: www.paulinefrancis.co.uk

Usborne Quicklinks

For links to websites where you can read private letters from Lady Jane Grey, learn more about her life and the rules of the Tudor court, and find out about the Catholic and Protestant struggle for the throne, go to the Usborne Quicklinks Website at www.usborne-quicklinks.com and enter the keywords "raven queen".

When using the Internet, make sure you follow the Internet safety guidelines displayed on the Usborne Quicklinks Website. Usborne Publishing is not responsible for the content on any website other than its own. We recommend that children are supervised while on the Internet, that they do not use Internet chat rooms, and that you use Internet filtering software to block unsuitable material. For more information, see the "Net Help" area on the Usborne Quicklinks website.

Usborne Publishing is not responsible and does not accept liability for the availability or content of any website other than its own, or for any exposure to harmful, offensive, or inaccurate material which may appear on the Web. Usborne Publishing will have no liability for any damage or loss caused by viruses that may be downloaded as a result of browsing the sites it recommends.

For more compelling tales of
love and courage
log on to
www.fiction.usborne.com

Edith Pattou

North Child

Superstition says that children born facing north will travel far from home and Rose's mother is terrified that Rose, a north child, will face a lonely, icy death if she follows her destiny. But Rose is unaware of this, so when an enormous white bear appears and wants to take her away she agrees to his bargain.

Rose travels on the bear's back to a mysterious castle where a silent stranger appears to her night after night. Overwhelmed by curiosity, Rose does something that has terrible consequences. Now she must embark on an epic journey to save the one she loves and fulfil her true destiny.

"A haunting, epic love story... It sweeps along with memorable grace." *TES Teacher*

ISBN 0 7460 6837 9

Nancy Butcher

Mirror, Mirror

Queen Veda is the most beautiful woman in the kingdom and that's the way she wants it to stay. So when she sends all the girls of the realm to a new academy where they are offered a beauty wonder pill, her daughter Princess Ana is suspicious. She has always had to hide her good looks to keep her mother's affection. So why is the Queen suddenly promoting beauty, when she has always been the fairest of them all?

Bringing a modern twist to a classic fairy story, *Mirror, Mirror* is a lyrical and absorbing tale that resonates strongly in today's looks-obsessed world.

ISBN 0 7460 7309 7

Meg Harper

Fur

Grace loves swimming in the sea: it soothes her when she's restless and comforts her when she's sad. Even her dreams are full of the scents and sounds of the ocean.

But dark shadows are troubling the peaceful waters of Grace's life. Her body is beginning to change but *not* as she expected. And now that she's started seeing Nik, will she be able to keep her secret to herself?

Mystery and myth intertwine in this thoroughly modern story of body image and first love.

"An enchanting, well-written novel."
School Librarian

ISBN 0 7460 6749 6

3 8002 01502 2298